Blueb~~~~
and Murder

Holly Holmes Cozy Culinary Mystery –
book 5

K.E. O'Connor

K.E. O'Connor Books

BLUEBERRY BLAST AND MURDER

ISBN: 978-1-9163573-4-1

Written by K.E. O'Connor

Edited by Amy Hart

Cover design by Stunning Book Covers

Beta read by my wonderful early review team. You're all amazing.

Chapter 1

I paused from loading the trolley on the back of my delivery bike as several wedding fair stallholders hurried past, their arms laden with stunning displays of flowers, the air alive with a heady floral scent.

"Woof, woof?" Meatball, my adorable corgi cross, bounced around my feet, wagging his tail.

"It's all go here again." I petted his head. "Is this wedding business making you think about finding the love of your life?"

He licked my hand, adoration in his large dark eyes.

I grinned and gave him a quick cuddle. "I feel the same. We don't need anyone else to be happy. You're my furry soulmate."

"Holly! Save me." Princess Alice Audley dashed across the courtyard, her long blonde hair flying out behind her and her cheeks flushed.

"What's the matter?" I looked over her shoulder. Was she being chased?

"It's my miserable cousin, Diana. Honestly, talk about a downer. She hasn't cracked a smile since she's been here. All she wants to do is talk about how awful men are now she's done with love. It's dismal."

I grinned and turned my attention to the trolley, securing the boxes of blueberry blast muffins on the back. "You can hardly blame her. She has just separated from her husband."

Alice gave a dramatic sigh. "You'd think it was the end of the world, not simply a failed marriage. Their relationship has been on the rocks for ages. Remember that enormous wedding anniversary celebration they had here? Even I could tell something was wrong between them." She sidled over to the bike. "What have you got in the boxes?"

"Nothing for you." I rested a hand on the top box. "I'm making a delivery to Artfully Homewares. Catherine is hosting a private party this afternoon and asked us to cater for it."

"I'm sure she won't mind if one cake is missing." Alice's hand crept toward the box.

I tapped the back of her hand. "You may be a princess, but you don't get to steal someone else's treats."

She huffed out a breath. "Very well. I'm much more excited about seeing your medieval decorated cake, anyway. How many layers has it got?"

I grinned at the mention of my baking. I'd been working on the cake for days, designing decorations and deciding on the final color scheme. "Five layers. It's looking good."

"It had better taste as good as it looks," Alice said. "And I want the first piece, since you're depriving me of these treats."

"The wedding fair will be open soon. There'll be loads of businesses giving away cake samples to lure people in. You can have your fill there."

"It won't be as delicious as yours. And I can't eat cake on my own in public. Imagine the headlines in the society pages: '*Princess Alice and Her Dismal Love Life.*' '*Princess Turns to Food for Comfort Because No One Will*

Marry Her.' And the pictures will show me stuffing myself with cake, all because I can't find a man."

"Maybe you'll get inspiration on how to find the perfect man at the wedding fair."

Alice turned and stared at the large marquees set up in the castle's grounds. "When I get married, I'm doing it barefoot on a beach, somewhere hot, where no one knows who I am. I'm not having all this fuss."

"I thought you wanted a huge wedding."

"I've changed my mind."

"Your parents won't approve. They'll want the wedding here." I gestured at Audley Castle. It was one of the prettiest castles in the country and had held a fair few grand weddings.

"So they can show me off like a prize peacock. All they care about is the connections my future husband will have." She scowled at the marquees. "What about love? Isn't that what marriage is supposed to be about?"

I adjusted the cake boxes. I was no expert when it came to love. I'd been single a long time. It usually didn't bother me, but seeing the wedding paraphernalia, it got me wondering. Maybe it was time I found a guy.

Meatball bounced off his front paws, his gaze on the trolley of treats.

"Meatball thinks you're being cruel by depriving us of those cakes," Alice said. "We can share one. I'm always happy to share with Meatball."

"You two can beg as much as you like. You're not getting these cakes. Here, have one of these." I passed her a leaflet.

"Plogging? Is this a spelling mistake?"

"No. It's something that started in Scandinavia. You combine jogging with cleaning up the countryside. It's popular over there. I'm planning an event after the wedding fair has finished. I thought we could get a few groups together and have a gentle jog around the beautiful countryside and make sure it's litter free. You're welcome to join in."

Her nose wrinkled. "I'm not a fan of running, or anything that makes me all sweaty and gross."

"It'll be gentle. You won't get a chance to go fast because you'll be stopping to pick up litter. You can get fit and clean up the environment."

"It doesn't sound too terrible," Alice said. "Okay, I'm in."

"You can be on my team. I'm hoping to recruit more people from the village. I figured I'd put up these leaflets and get some sign-ups. I'm already up to fifty. And I'll bake treats for people to eat at the end of the run. It'll be an incentive to get involved."

"Run! You said gentle jogging only." Alice's eyes narrowed. "You're not trying to trick me into some hideous extreme sport?"

I laughed. "Never. It'll be very gentle jogging. No sweating almost guaranteed."

"I could issue a decree so everyone in the village has to take part," Alice said.

"I'm hoping people will be happy to volunteer since it's for such a good cause," I said. "But if I'm low on numbers, I'll come back to you on the forced villager involvement."

"I'll be happy to twist arms. Well, get my security to do the rough stuff." She looked longingly at the boxes of cake. "Are you going to the catwalk event?"

"Nope. One wedding dress looks the same as all the others."

"No! You must come. I'm taking Diana, although I think it'll be a pointless exercise. I can't bear the thought of spending the evening with her while she cries over wedding dresses and her terrible marriage."

"So you want to burden me with that delight as well?"

Alice grinned at me. "That's what friends are for. We can share each other's pain. Plus, there'll be free champagne and canapés."

"I know! The kitchen is providing those canapés."

"Which means the food will be amazing. Come with me and Diana tomorrow evening. Between us, we can cheer her up. What else have you got planned?"

"Um, watching a cookery program?" I didn't exactly have a jam-packed social life.

"You can watch that any time. And if you get bored, you can always leave."

I sighed. Alice was hard to dissuade when she set her mind to something. "Sure. My exciting plans can wait."

"I'll get us front row seats," Alice said. "We can fill our faces with delicious food and laugh at all the flouncy gowns."

"It's a date. Now, I'd better get a move on. I need to get these cakes to Catherine." I scooped up Meatball, secured him in the basket on the front of the bike, and settled his safety helmet on his head.

"Bring me back a cake," Alice said. "I can smell how delicious they are."

"Go ask Chef Heston for a treat." I slung my leg over the bike. "I'll see you later." I pushed off and rounded the corner. I slammed on the brakes and a gasp shot out of me.

"Get your hands off me, you enormous oaf." A red-faced, red-haired woman was being held securely by Campbell Milligan, the castle's head of security.

"You've been warned before. I told you not to come back." Campbell strode along, tugging the woman beside him.

"You don't own this place. I can come here if I like. I paid the visitor entry fee. I haven't even had a chance to look around the wedding fair."

"You're not welcome."

"What's going on?" I asked as I wheeled my bike toward them.

"It's nothing to do with you." Campbell glanced at me, his stern features hardening.

"Get him off me," the woman said. "I'm innocent. He's being a bully."

I knew Campbell well enough to know he'd never bully anyone. I cycled along beside them. "Campbell can be protective of the family. Did you do something to upset them?"

"I'm not interested in the Audley family or this tedious drafty castle," the woman said.

"Then why is he making you leave?" I asked.

"Holly, go about your business. It looks like you have a delivery to make." Campbell glared at me.

"I do. But we're heading in the same direction. I can keep you company." And find out why he was dragging this angry woman to the exit.

"Not anymore we aren't." He abruptly turned and headed toward a different exit.

I put my foot on the ground as he strode away, the woman still complaining as he tugged her along. I was impressed by the fight she was putting up. Campbell was twice her size and not to be messed with.

I was just pushing off again to head into the village, when I spotted a tall, elegant woman wearing large dark glasses, a green scarf over her hair. I could have been mistaken, but it looked like she'd been watching the argument between Campbell and the woman. Although now, she seemed focused on me.

I slowly raised a hand. There was something familiar about her. Did I know her? It was hard to see her features from this distance.

The second she saw me lift my hand, she turned and disappeared around the side of the castle.

If she was up to no good, Campbell would soon be chasing her down as well. There were so many people here as part of the wedding fair that it wasn't unusual to find them lost and confused, stumbling into places they shouldn't.

"Let's get a move on, Meatball. It'll be good to get away from this chaos for an hour."

"Woof, woof!" His bark was full of agreement as we headed out of the castle gates and along the empty lanes toward Audley St. Mary, my pretty village home.

Although I often complained about the hills that led into the village, I always got a good workout when I used the bike to make deliveries. The burn in my thighs told me my muscles were definitely working hard today.

Meatball loved being in the bike basket. He was secured inside so he couldn't jump out, but he could sit back, place his front paws over the front of the basket and get an excellent view as I cycled along.

I waved at several villagers as I headed toward the stores. Audley St. Mary had a great range of small independent stores that had a thriving trade. There were a few chain stores and restaurants, one of which was a café I never entered, considering it put my own café out of business not so long ago.

And that was where I was headed. My former café was home to Artfully Homewares, and I was happy to see it thriving.

I stopped the bike and climbed off. I unbuckled my helmet and flipped it over the handles of the bike, scooped Meatball out, and removed his helmet, before placing him on the ground.

"Holly! What are you doing away from the castle?"

I turned at the sound of Lord Rupert Audley's voice and smiled at him. "I've got a delivery to make. What about you?"

He sighed and stuffed his hands into his pockets. "I'm hiding."

"From what?"

"Ever since the wedding fair started, I've had several long, intensely awkward conversations with my mother. She keeps talking about my wedding."

I gritted my teeth and winced. "Your wedding! Is there someone you're interested in marrying?"

"Several eligible bachelorettes have been mentioned," Rupert said glumly.

My stomach flip-flopped. I'd had a bit of a crush on Rupert for a long time. "Have any of these bachelorettes taken your eye?"

"They're all lovely girls, but not what I'm interested in." He glanced at me and pushed his messy blond hair off his face. "I mean, I know I need to settle down. Grow up, as my mother keeps telling me, but why can't things stay the same? We're happy as we are, aren't we?"

"I mean, sure. You seem happy enough. Although maybe you could meet someone who'll make you happier."

He grinned. "You make me happy. Especially when you come laden with delicious looking treats in boxes."

I chuckled and shook my head. "No chance. Your sister tried to pull the same stunt when she saw these cakes. This is a delivery for Catherine in the pottery store."

"Oh! Well, why don't we both go in? We can have a browse while we're here."

"I can't be long. I need to get back to the castle. I'm making the finishing touches to my medieval cake design."

"Alice was telling me all about that. It sounds exciting. Can't you spare half an hour away from the kitchen? You deserve a break. I bet Chef Heston's been working you too hard as usual."

"He always does." Being around Rupert put a smile on my face. He was always thinking about other people and making sure they were happy. "You're right. Half an hour won't hurt."

"I'll give you a hand in with the boxes." Rupert unclipped the boxes and lifted up two.

I grabbed the rest, and we headed into the store, Meatball trotting beside me.

Catherine Miquel looked up from her position behind the reclaimed oak counter, the counter I had fitted when this was my café. She had warm brown eyes, a friendly smile, and often had a paintbrush tucked behind one ear. "Holly! And ... goodness. Lord Rupert. This is an unexpected surprise. Do you normally make deliveries for the castle, your ... lordship?"

He chuckled. "This is a special occasion. And call me Rupert. I'm just helping Holly out."

Catherine's eyes widened as she looked at me. "That's nice of you. Come through the back, you can put the cakes in the kitchen."

I grinned. "I know the way. Is it okay to have Meatball in here? He's well-behaved. He probably thinks of this place as a second home."

"Of course. He's welcome." Catherine strode ahead of us, holding open the doors so we could get through with the boxes.

Although the place had a familiar feel, it looked so different. Catherine had painted the walls a bright yellow and added extra shelving in the front for the pots people could make in the store. There was also a large display cabinet at the back and the counter had been moved.

When I entered the kitchen, I was surprised to see a large kiln in one corner.

I set the boxes down, my gaze roving over the room. It was different, but I approved. A lot of care and love had gone into making this place beautiful.

"Thanks for bringing these over," Catherine said. "One of the ladies in the village is having a birthday party here this afternoon. She said she wanted some extra special treats. Of course, I instantly thought of the castle kitchen and all the delicious desserts you make."

"I'm glad you did," Rupert said. "Holly's the best baker we've ever had. We plan to make sure she stays with us forever."

I glanced at him and grinned. "You're very kind. Everyone else in the kitchen is also capable of making nice cakes."

"Oh, absolutely! You just do those special finishing touches that make your cakes magic," Rupert said.

"I'm thrilled to have the cakes for the party," Catherine said. "Have you got time to stop for a cup of tea?"

"We hoped you'd say that." Rupert rubbed his hands together. "And I wouldn't mind having a go at painting a pot while I'm here."

Catherine's hand fluttered against her chest. "Of course. It would be my honor to host you."

"Only if it's no bother," I said. "You do have the party to sort out."

"It's no trouble. The party doesn't start for another few hours. I'm almost set up and ready to go. You're welcome to try your hand at pottery painting. Would you like to try, too, Holly?"

"I would. Thanks."

"We came for a look around not long after you opened," Rupert said. "I brought my sister and Holly. Alice was showing off her painting skills, so I didn't get a look in when it came to having a go."

"I remember." Catherine brewed up tea and set out some mugs. "Your sister's visit to the store drew quite an audience."

"She always does that," Rupert said. "She's a right show off."

"I was grateful for the publicity." Catherine poured the tea. "We were on the front page of the newspapers for several weeks, and I've been booked solid ever since. An endorsement from the Audley family is always good for business."

"Well, I suppose Alice has her uses." Rupert accepted a mug of tea.

I nodded a thanks at Catherine as she passed me a mug. "It looks like the store's doing really well."

"It is. I'm thrilled," Catherine said. "I always dreamed of owning my own pottery and homeware store. I couldn't miss the opportunity when I discovered this place. And the villagers have been so welcoming."

"It's why I love it here," I said.

"Let me take you through to the store." Catherine walked to the kitchen door. "You can have a look at the pots available for painting. I'll bring out a few of these cakes for you to enjoy as well."

Rupert grinned like an overexcited child. "That sounds perfect. Come on, Holly." He took hold of my arm and guided me into the store.

I didn't miss the surprised look on Catherine's face as he escorted me out.

My relationship with the Audley family was unique. I considered myself privileged to be included in their friendship group but understood how odd it seemed to others. A kitchen assistant being friends with a lord and a princess. Sometimes, I couldn't get my head around it, either. But it just worked.

We were soon settled at the table, paint brushes in hand, cakes beside us, and two small pots awaiting their final design. Meatball was settled by my feet.

"This is the life," Rupert said. "This is all I need to be happy. A strong mug of tea, a delicious cake, and you."

My eyebrows shot up. "Me?"

He glanced up, his cheeks flaming. "I mean, a good friend. You understand? I mean, you're not just a friend. You're ... well, you're special. You make Audley Castle special."

I looked away, my gaze going to Meatball, who sat patiently by the table, no doubt hoping for some cake. "How about we paint these pots?"

"Yes. Right. Let's get to work." He grinned and ducked his head.

If only I could date Rupert. Although if I did, life would get a lot more complicated, and I was happy with my current situation.

Cake, tea, and my best furry buddy by my side. It wasn't a bad way to live.

Chapter 2

My work back at the castle kitchen kept me busy for the rest of the day after my time with Rupert. My pot was drying at the store, and I'd be able to pick it up in a few days.

My apron was hung up, and I was heading out the back door toward my apartment with Meatball, when raised voices made me slow.

"You should have told the truth." An elegantly dressed woman with a neat gray bob jabbed a finger at the woman standing opposite her. "You stole that design. You must have seen it on my website."

The other woman laughed sharply. She was a head shorter, petite, with dark hair, and dressed in a cream suit. "You'd never come up with that design. Everything you show is three seasons out of date."

"That's not true. I've been in this business a lot longer than you. Classic designs never go out of style."

"You're past your prime. Maybe it's time you retired."

The taller woman stepped forward. "I would if I could. You have no right to take what isn't yours."

"I have plenty of ideas of my own. I don't need to steal them from some washed up bitter harpy."

I sucked in a breath. This was getting nasty. Should I intervene?

The shorter woman staggered to one side and clutched her stomach.

The other woman extended a hand as if to help her. "Are you sick?"

She waved away the comment. "I'm fine. There's nothing wrong with me."

"If you weren't sampling the free champagne at these events, you'd have a clear enough head to do your own work," the gray-haired woman said. "You used to be much better than this."

"There's nothing wrong with my work. And I could say the same for you. Those banners you brought to this event are the same as last year's. What's the matter? The money not coming in?"

"You worry about your own business. I'm doing just fine."

The other woman staggered again. She did look unsteady on her feet. "Stay away from me. Take your tired old banners and your boring wedding flowers and leave me alone." The dark-haired woman turned, wobbling as she did so, before she walked away.

"Come on, Meatball. Let's see what that was all about." I patted my leg, and he trotted along beside me until we reached the tall woman.

She was muttering under her breath as we approached. She turned and her eyes narrowed when she saw me. "May I help you?"

"Actually, I was wondering if I could help you. I couldn't help but hear you arguing with that other woman. Is everything okay?"

She waved a hand in the air, her shoulders tight around her ears. "Just the usual professional rivalry. Connie thinks she should be the only wedding florist at this event. It's ridiculous. There are hundreds of potential clients here. She can't have them all."

"You're a florist?"

She glanced at me before letting out a sigh and extending her hand. "That's right. I'm Belinda Adler. I've been in the business thirty years. Sometimes, I can't believe it's been that long."

I shook her outstretched hand. "Holly Holmes. I work in the castle's kitchen. I do the baking for the café and provide some food for the family, usually the desserts."

Belinda's thin eyebrows rose. "That must keep you busy. What a fabulous place to work."

"I enjoy it. I suppose you're used to seeing places like this. The wedding fairs must take you all over the country."

"They do." She looked at the castle. "After all this time, I barely notice where I am."

"You don't enjoy doing the fairs?"

Her lips pursed. "I used to. But maybe Connie's right. I should think about retiring. Wedding planning is a young person's game. You need a ton of energy to keep up with the increasing demands of clients."

"Is Connie the woman you were arguing with?"

"Yes, Connie Barber. And, as much as it pains me to say this, she's an excellent florist. At least, she used to be. I don't know what's happened, but in the last six months, her designs have gone downhill. She used to be a perfectionist. Everything had to be pristine and perfectly color matched. I was taking a look at her offerings at the fair today, and her work was shoddy."

"I couldn't help but notice she was unsteady on her feet. Is she unwell?"

"I think everyone is noticing that. It's a stressful business, weddings. Connie is coping by drinking too much. Everyone has an idea about what their perfect day will be like. If you don't pull it off or tell them it's not possible, there's hell to pay. I've lost count of the number of times I've been screamed at by some mad-eyed bride who didn't get her dream wedding flowers."

"It doesn't sound like you enjoy the business of weddings anymore."

She twisted the gold band on her ring finger. "When I was younger, I loved seeing everything come together. My beautiful flowers would make the big day something special. Now, I don't know, things have changed. I've been wondering if it's time for me to change, too."

"Why not? I did that when I came to work at the castle."

Belinda tilted her head. "How did you do that?"

"I studied history at university and had plans to teach, but it never worked out and I struggled to find paid work. As a sideline, I also studied catering. Then I opened a café in Audley St. Mary."

"That must have been exciting. It didn't work out?"

"It did for a while, but as you said, running your own business is stressful. There's always a competitor snapping at your heels. Or in my case, a giant chain café that moved in, offered discounted coffees and muffins, and gobbled up my profit."

"I'm sorry to hear that," Belinda said. "I always choose an independent café. I don't even mind paying a bit more for my muffins. They're always nicer when they haven't been shipped in from some warehouse and simply re-heated."

I wrinkled my nose. "I'd never do that. I used to bake fresh every day. Sadly, not enough people thought the same as you. I was getting ready to close down my café, when I saw the job to work in the kitchen at Audley Castle. I was intrigued. Now, I get to be here every day and make amazing cakes."

Belinda's shoulders sagged, and she shook her head. "I admire your courage. You're much younger than me, though. I can't change now."

"Of course you can," I said. "There must be something else you want to do. If wedding flowers aren't your thing, you could specialize in flowers for different sorts of parties."

"Like funerals? Hardly a cheery job change. And I'd be surrounded by lilies, and their pollen stains my skin."

"What about baptisms or bar mitzvahs?"

She shook her head. "I'd face the same challenges. I'll hang on in here for a few more years, then maybe look into selling the business. I wish I had your pluck and youth. Unfortunately, an old dog can't learn new tricks." She nodded at me. "Nice talking to you, Holly. I needed a friendly face after confronting Connie."

"You're welcome." I watched as Belinda strode away, her back straight and her arms swinging by her sides. I felt a little sorry for her, trapped in a profession she no longer enjoyed, and fighting with other florists over wedding designs and customers.

I looked down at Meatball. "Do you agree? Do you think an old dog can't learn new tricks?"

He bounced on his paws and wagged his tail.

"That's what I think, too. A dog can learn a trick if he wants to, given enough treats and encouragement. Come on, let's go get some dinner."

I was heading into work with Meatball by my heels the next morning, when his ears pricked and his tail shot up.

I looked around, expecting to see Alice. He always got excited when she was about. Instead, a tiny dog, dressed in a bright pink onesie, with a little fluffy hat on its head, bounded toward us.

Meatball barked before he bounced over to the dog.

I hurried after him. I wasn't worried about Meatball being aggressive, but he could be overenthusiastic when it came to making friends, and this dog was tiny. I could probably balance it on one hand.

"Hello, who are you?" I said to the little pink cutie pie.

The dog froze, its eyes large as it spied Meatball. It yipped and began to growl.

I grinned. Typical Chihuahua. They were tiny in body but had the heart of a lion.

I kneeled and held my hand out. "You don't need to worry about us. I'm friendly, so is Meatball. Where's your owner?" I let the dog sniff my fingers, and slowly its growling subsided.

Meatball sniffed all around the dog. His gaze went to mine as he snuffled around the onesie.

"I won't dress you up any time soon." I always thought it was a strange thing to do, dress an animal. Unless they had no fur, it was freezing cold, or they were sick, they didn't need designer onesies to keep warm.

I scratched between the dog's ears, twisting the collar around to read the nametags. "Saffron. That's a very pretty name."

"There you are! You naughty girl. You shouldn't run away from me." I recognized the woman from yesterday. It was Connie.

I stood as she approached. "Does she belong to you?"

Connie scowled at Saffron. "Yes! She's so badly behaved. She's always running off. Saffron, you're a naughty girl."

Saffron's tail lowered between her back legs.

"She's probably overexcited because of the wedding fair. She's such a small dog, all this noise and commotion must be overwhelming."

Connie pursed her lips. "That's rubbish. She's been to plenty of wedding fairs. She just doesn't like taking orders. You bad, bad girl."

I frowned. That was no way to talk to a dog. Positive reinforcement and plenty of treats got things done. "I'm sure she didn't mean it." My gaze ran over Connie. There was a sallow tinge to her skin, and she had dark circles under her eyes. "I hope you don't mind me asking, but are you feeling okay?"

She pressed her fingers against her forehead. "No, I feel dreadful. Everyone's coming down with a stomach bug at this fair."

"I didn't know there was a stomach bug going around."

"Most of the models in the catwalk event this evening have come down with it. And when I woke this morning, I could barely get out of bed. I had a thumping headache and my stomach was twisting into knots, but I couldn't leave my stand all day. My assistant hasn't been with me for long." Connie sighed and kneeled. "And I could really do without Saffron misbehaving. It's only making me stressed."

Saffron backed away, the whites of her eyes showing.

Connie grabbed the dog. "Stop being so difficult."

Saffron yelped and cowered in Connie's arms.

The poor sweetie was shaking. "Maybe you shouldn't —"

"I can't stop. The wedding fair is opening soon." Connie turned and strode away.

Meatball whined and lifted one paw in the air.

"Someone got out of the wrong side of the bed this morning. Poor Saffron. She's taking the brunt of it because her mom's not feeling well." I gave him a hearty belly rub before we headed to the kitchen so I could get on with the day's long list of baking.

When I got a moment, I'd pull Connie to one side and suggest dog training classes. Saffron was only misbehaving because she hadn't received the proper training. And if Connie kept yelling at her, things would only get worse for both of them, and I couldn't stand the thought of an unhappy dog.

I looked down at Meatball. "We need to take Saffron under our wing. That way, maybe we can make them both happy."

"Woof, woof!"

I smiled. "Clever boy. You're always right about these things. First the baking, then the behavioral classes."

Chapter 3

I'd just taken a large tray of blueberry blast muffins out of the oven and set it on the counter to cool, when Alice and Diana walked into the kitchen.

"We're going to the wedding fair, and you're coming with us." There was a gleam of desperation in Alice's eyes.

I nodded at Lady Diana, whose eyes were red-rimmed. She didn't acknowledge me. "I wish I could. I'm a bit behind on the baking."

Alice wagged a finger in the air as she shook her head. "No, no, no. I insist on it. You must come with us."

"I would if I could." I gestured at the oven. "The café is rammed to bursting point. Chef Heston is almost pulling his hair out."

"You leave him to me. Diana, wait here and try not to drip tears on the cakes." Alice strode away.

Lady Diana sniffed, her shoulders hunched forward.

I shifted from foot to foot and bit my bottom lip. I didn't know Lady Diana well. She'd been to the castle a few times since I'd started working here. The last time, she'd been focused on her anniversary party and had barely spared me a glance.

"I don't suppose you've got any chocolate, have you?" Her voice was low and toneless.

"Of course. Would you like some?"

She sniffed again. "All I want to do is stay under my duvet and eat chocolate. Alice dragged me out today. She said it would do me good."

"If chocolate is what you need, then I can help." I raced to the chiller cabinet. My gaze shifted from the salted caramel chocolate sponge to the triple chocolate ganache before settling on my three layer rocky road with melted mocha chocolate fudge and marshmallows. I selected two large slices and set them in front of Lady Diana.

She lifted a piece and took an enormous bite, leaving a smear of chocolate either side of her mouth.

"I know it's not my place to say, but I'm very sorry about what happened between you and your husband. Maybe it's just a temporary blip."

She gave a most unladylike grunt and stuffed more rocky road into her mouth.

"If you ever need more comforting treats, just come find me in the kitchen."

She chewed and swallowed. "Thanks. Actually, this has made me feel marginally better."

"It's all arranged." Alice walked across the kitchen. "Chef Heston is letting you take your lunch break now."

"Alice, I don't want you getting me in trouble." Chef Heston had warned me several times about not spending too much time with the family.

"He's hardly going to refuse me. Come along now. And Diana, wipe that chocolate off your face."

Lady Diana wiped a hand across the back of her mouth. She picked up the other piece of rocky road and began to eat.

Alice shook her head. "You're a lost cause. Shoulders back and put a smile on your face. Let's go and look around the wedding fair."

"It's like you're trying to torture me," Lady Diana muttered.

"It'll do you good," Alice said. "We can sample cake, try champagne, and imagine we're blushing brides-to-be."

"I once was a blushing bride-to-be." Lady Diana slouched along beside us as we headed out the kitchen and over to the marquees.

"And you will be again, one day," Alice said. "You just need to get better at picking the right man."

"Look who's talking."

Alice stiffened beside me. "At least I don't have a failed marriage."

"No, you have two failed engagements."

"Why don't we just try to enjoy this wedding fair?" I sensed a huge argument brewing and wasn't keen on being in the middle of it.

Lady Diana grunted again, and Alice squeezed my elbow tightly.

We headed into the first marquee, and I was delighted to see this one was full of food and drink. That's what I was interested in. The flowers, the gowns, and the wedding accessories didn't interest me.

When I got married, if I got married, there'd be a magnificent banquet of food and drink for my guests. That was where I'd lavish my attention.

"Where shall we start?" Alice's eyes gleamed as she looked at the stalls laden with free samples and tempting chocolate treats.

I caught her eye, and we grinned at each other. "Straight to the desserts?"

"I need some champagne," Lady Diana said.

"It's barely noon," Alice said.

Lady Diana shrugged. "I need something to fortify myself if you're going to drag me around this fair."

Alice shook her head. "You go and find some champagne. I'll be with Holly over by the cakes."

"Don't leave me on my own. Look, this chap has got plenty of alcohol. He'll give us some samples." Lady Diana grabbed Alice's arm and tugged her over to a large display that boasted the best Merlot you'll ever taste.

I followed close behind, dodging through the crowds as the hordes of eager-eyed brides hunted for their perfect wedding caterer.

A tall, classically handsome man in his mid-forties with dark hair held out two full glasses of something sparkling to Alice and Lady Diana. "It's an honor to have you here, ladies. I'm Bruce Osman. I own Osman Vineyard. Have you ever tasted my tongue tantalizing creations?"

"No, but I need some now." Lady Diana was quick to snag one of the glasses.

Bruce smiled broadly and held out the other glass to Alice. "Princess? May I tempt you?"

"Just a sip." Alice took the glass. "We're more interested in the cake."

"You'll find my champagne goes well with all manner of sweet treats," he said. His gaze drifted over me before he focused back on Alice and Lady Diana.

I smirked. I clearly wasn't pulling off the 'I'm special, too' vibe today. I glanced down and noticed I still had my work apron on. That would do it.

"Holly needs a glass, too," Alice said.

"Of course, Princess." Bruce swept into action, filling a glass and passing it to me.

I nodded my thanks and took the tiniest of sips. I had an afternoon of baking ahead of me and needed a clear head so I didn't mix the ingredients incorrectly.

"Bruce, darling. Do you mind if I borrow the—" A pretty blonde woman in a tight red suit stared with widening eyes at Alice. "Oh my goodness! You're Princess Alice Audley."

Bruce's eyes tightened a fraction before he nodded. "Come back later, Zoe. I need to give my special customers my full attention."

Zoe's red painted lips opened and closed a few times. "Ladies, if you're looking for anyone to plan your wedding, come to my display. I'm in the next marquee. Zoe Rossini. I'm the best wedding planner in the county."

Lady Diana downed the champagne and thumped the empty glass on the table.

"That's very kind of you." Alice smiled sweetly. "We're making our way into that marquee a little later."

Zoe grinned and clasped her hands together. "I'll give you a special discount. In return, if you could simply pose for—"

"That's enough, Zoe. These ladies don't need any sales patter. I'm sure they know how to make a well-informed decision." Bruce's tone had turned sharp, and the warmth in his eyes had been replaced by an icy glare.

Zoe pressed her lips together. "Don't forget me." She turned and hurried away.

Bruce spread his arms out. "What else can I tempt you with? I'm sure such sophisticated ladies know their way around all the classic reds. I have a fruity Sauvignon that'll bring a glow to your pretty cheeks."

"I'll have more champagne," Lady Diana said.

"Of course." Bruce immediately refilled her glass. "You have excellent taste."

"Steady on," Alice whispered to her. "You don't want to make a scene and fall over because you've had too much to drink."

"I don't care if I do. Weddings are a sham. This whole thing is a joke. Half the people who get married after this event will be divorced before they've lasted ten years. I didn't even manage five. Marriage is for losers."

"Marriage isn't for everyone, but it does bring some people joy," Bruce said smoothly.

"Are you married?" Lady Diana asked.

"There is a special someone in my life. I have proposed to her," he said.

"Then you're living a lie. She'll break your heart. You should get out while you can," Lady Diana said.

"That's enough of that." Alice yanked the glass out of Lady Diana's hand. "My apologies, Mr. Osman. My cousin is having a hard time."

"No need to apologize. Weddings can be stressful."

"As can a divorce," Lady Diana muttered.

"You need some air," Alice said to her.

"I need more champagne," Lady Diana said.

"Tough luck. This way." Alice dragged Lady Diana out of the marquee.

I placed my glass down and looked longingly at the food. I'd have to come back another time when I didn't have a depressed member of the Audley family with me.

"Let's go take a look at the flowers," Alice said as I emerged from the marquee. "You like those, Diana."

Lady Diana simply shrugged, but allowed Alice to lead her into the next marquee, while I followed behind them.

The heady floral smell in the air almost made me sneeze. The place was a riot of color and noise, full of flower arrangers and wedding planners courting potential customers.

A high-pitched yip had me turning. I spotted Saffron, Connie's dog, her leash looped under a chair leg so she couldn't get away.

Connie appeared a few seconds later. She spoke to a younger woman with pale pink hair pulled off her face in a low ponytail and a camera around her neck.

The younger woman stepped back, her expression tightening, suggesting Connie had just insulted her.

Connie ducked down, grabbed Saffron, and held her out to a much older woman who'd just arrived, her gray hair loose and flowing down her back.

"Let's check out this stall." I led Alice and Lady Diana to Connie's flower stand.

Connie turned, a tight smile on her face. It morphed into a megawatt display when she spotted Alice. "Welcome to Florally Forever. I produce the finest wedding bouquets and decorations to befit royalty. It's my pleasure that you've come to inspect my offerings, Princess Alice."

"It was Holly's idea to take a look," Alice said. "Your flowers are pretty."

"That's kind of you to say." Connie glanced at the two women standing beside her and waved them away. "Is there anything in particular you'd like to see?"

Alice glanced at me. "We'll just take a general look."

"Hello, again," I said. "It's good to see Saffron hasn't made any more escape attempts."

Connie frowned at me. "She hasn't been able to. I've made sure she can't get away."

"Is that little dog yours?" Alice looked over as Saffron was carried away by the older woman. "She's so cute. She's tiny."

"She may be tiny, but she's very naughty. I thought she'd calm down once she got older, but she's getting worse. People warned me not to get a Chihuahua, but I figured she was the perfect size to bring with me when I worked."

"Perhaps she'd benefit from some training," I said. "When Meatball was younger, I took him to weekly classes for almost a year."

"Meatball?" Connie asked.

"Holly's dog. He's adorable. Although he does have a bit of a naughty streak," Alice said.

"He does his best," I said. "Perhaps he could spend some time with Saffron. He's very friendly with other dogs. She might learn a few things from him."

"Saffron doesn't like other dogs. She prefers to be with me." Connie's attention returned to Princess Alice. "May I offer you a complimentary flower arrangement? You could put it inside the castle for everyone to admire."

"Thanks, but no. We have someone who does our flowers," Alice said. "Most of them come from our own gardens."

Connie dabbed her top lip with her fingers. She pressed a hand against her stomach, a pained expression crossing her face.

"Is that stomach bug still bothering you?" I asked her.

She glared at me. "It's nothing. I'm fine. Everyone's got it."

I studied her complexion. I could be mistaken but her eyes had a yellow tinge. What kind of stomach bug made your eyes change color?

"Are you unwell?" Alice asked. "You do look a little peaky."

"It's nothing, Princess. I appreciate your concern. I need to soldier on. There are bouquets to make and orders to fulfill."

"It's important to look after yourself," Alice said.

"I'm ready for some cake now." Lady Diana plucked a flower off a bouquet on the display table. She squashed it in her fist.

"Don't do that!" Alice scooped up the bouquet. "You've spoiled it."

"It's fine, Princess. That one was just for show." Connie's mouth pinched together as she stared at the bouquet.

"No, I'll take this with me," Alice said. "I'll tell everyone where I got it from so you get lots of customers. My cousin isn't in the best of moods. It's making her thoughtless."

Lady Diana sighed and crossed her arms over her chest.

Connie's smile returned. "That would be wonderful. Take as many bouquets as you like."

"This one is just what I want," Alice said.

"Let's get cake," Lady Diana said. "And my feet hurt. I need to sit down."

"You're welcome to this brownie." Connie held up a plate. "I've been off my food this morning and just don't feel like it. It's all natural ingredients and freshly baked. Not by me. I can't cook to save my life."

"Thanks." Lady Diana took the brownie and ate it in three bites. "It was very sweet. I need more."

"That was the only one I had." Connie looked at the empty plate.

"Diana! You took this lady's last cake." Alice glared at her.

Lady Diana shrugged. "She offered it to me. Let's go find more cake."

"Oh, very well. So long as you promise to behave. No more spoiling displays or downing free champagne and complaining about failed marriages," Alice said.

"I'm promising nothing," Lady Diana said.

"Thanks for showing us your flowers," I said to Connie. "Let me know if you want Saffron and Meatball to have a doggie play date. I hope you feel better soon."

Connie barely spared me a glance. She handed Princess Alice a card. "If ever I can be of any service to you, here are my details."

Princess Alice nodded. "Thanks. I hope the wedding fair gets you a ton of orders."

As we headed out of the marquee, I glanced over my shoulder. Connie's face was sour as she spoke to the young woman with the pink hair again. I didn't much like the idea of working for Connie. I hoped she paid well to make up for her sharpness.

"I love flowers, cake, and champagne," Alice said. "If only we could have all those things without it involving a wedding and annoying men. Then it would be perfect."

"Men are so pointless," Lady Diana said.

"They're not all terrible. I know a few nice ones," Alice said.

"Name me one nice guy," Lady Diana said.

"My brother's nice."

Lady Diana grunted. "He doesn't count. He's family."

Alice glanced at me. "We have lots of lovely gardeners."

"Staff. Next."

"Campbell is very capable," Alice said.

Lady Diana sighed. "I knew you wouldn't be able to think of a single eligible bachelor who is decent, wealthy, honest, and kind."

"You're only saying that because your husband left you," Alice said.

Sensing a family row gathering force, I increased my pace. "No more talk of broken hearts. Let's go and enjoy some wedding cake."

And if Lady Diana's mouth was full of cake all the time, she wouldn't be able to argue with Alice. That sounded like a win-win all around.

Chapter 4

After the fun and games at the wedding fair with Alice and the increasingly sullen Lady Diana, who'd complained about feeling sick after eating so much cake, I'd spent the afternoon making fresh batches of blueberry blast muffins with whipped ginger cream. I had to ensure the café was stocked for the hungry mouths in need of a break after spending hours immersed in the world of weddings.

I welcomed the fresh air that hit me as I headed out of the kitchen and whistled for Meatball.

He bounced out of his kennel and sped after me. I usually walked him straight after work. It was a great way to get my thoughts together and unwind before dinner.

He trotted along in front of me, pausing now and again to sniff the ground.

"You'll have to entertain yourself this evening. I'm going to a catwalk."

He looked up at me, and his ears lowered.

"Don't worry, there aren't any actual cats there. Just lots of very pretty women wearing floating dresses and trying to convince me to buy an over-priced outfit I'll only ever wear once. I'd take you along, but you'd get bored. I know I will."

"Woof." He wagged his tail, a hopeful glint in his eyes.

"You'll be fine on your own for a couple of hours. I don't want to go, but Alice is insisting. And she needs me there to stop Lady Diana dragging down the mood. Even after a dozen cake samples, she refused to crack a smile."

Meatball's head shot around and his ears pricked.

I looked up and spotted the gray-haired woman from Connie's stand walking Saffron. They weren't that far ahead of us, so I increased my pace to catch up.

The woman turned as I drew near, and her gaze went to Meatball. "Sorry, but you need to keep your distance."

"Meatball's safe," I said.

"I'm not worried about him. This little one has a temper." She pointed at Saffron, who she'd reeled in on her lead. Saffron's growl could already be heard.

"They've met before," I said. "Saffron got away from Connie and I found her. She came nose to nose with Meatball."

The woman's eyebrows shot up. "And he lived to tell the tale?"

I smiled. "It was a close call. Saffron quickly put him in his place with plenty of growling. I think she was surprised that Meatball gave her a good sniffing."

"She can give a nasty nip if you don't look out." The woman's shoulders eased down. "I'm Misty Gilchrist. I look after Saffron and a number of the other dogs here while the ladies are working."

"Nice to meet you. I'm Holly Holmes. I work in the kitchen. This is my dog, Meatball."

Misty knelt on the ground and held her hand out to Meatball. "He's a gorgeous little fellow. Have you had him long?"

"Years. We go everywhere together. Well, I can't have him in the kitchen when I'm working, but he stays in his kennel right outside."

Misty gave him a pet, which he thoroughly enjoyed, his tail wagging wildly.

The whole time she was petting Meatball, Saffron was growling, a sullen look on her furry face.

"That's enough from you, madam." Misty stepped back and stroked Saffron. "She's so highly strung. I take her for long walks to try to calm her down, but being around Connie means she's often stressed."

"I noticed Connie looked stressed today when we met at the wedding fair." I gestured toward the woods, and we walked alongside each other. I made sure to keep Meatball away from Saffron in case she was tempted to take a chunk out of him.

Misty sighed. "Connie's a great boss, but she gets so tense about these events. Recently, she's been struggling. That's why she's taken on Leanna. You may have seen her at the stand as well. She's a sweet girl."

"Was that the young woman with the pink hair?"

Misty grinned. "That's right. Connie hates Leanna's hair color and keeps trying to get her to dye it. She said it's not suitable for a florist, but I think it's pretty. Leanna deals with pink things every day working with flowers, so why not have pink hair to match?"

"I thought it suited her," I said. "How long have you worked with Connie?"

"She contacted me to help with Saffron eight months ago. I haven't always done this, but when I retired from teaching, I reinvented myself. I love dogs so decided to do something with them. I've built a nice business specializing in doggy day care for the wedding industry. There are a lot of women who work in this field who have dogs, usually the kind you can pop into a purse and walk around with. They keep them company and aren't hard work, but they can't always have them at their displays.

For some strange reason, some people don't like dogs." Misty chuckled and shook her head.

"I've never figured that one out." We shared a smile. "That's a niche business. Doggy day care for wedding planners."

"It is, but I'm looking after four dogs while I'm here, so it's worth doing. And I travel in my campervan, so I don't have to pay for accommodation while I'm here. As you can imagine, there's plenty of money to be made in weddings, and these ladies are happy to pay me to look after their darling dogs while they work."

"I like the sound of that. It seems like the ideal job."

"I think it is. I'll never get rich doing it, but you don't work with animals for the money. And not only that, I get to see some amazing places. Wedding fairs are held at such beautiful locations across the country."

"I agree. I love working in the castle every day."

"It's a stunning place," Misty said. "I was admiring your flower meadow when I was walking Saffron this morning. I prefer a wildflower meadow over the cut flowers Connie has on her display. There's something so magical and untamed about them."

"If ever I marry, I want a bouquet full of wild flowers."

"You're not married?" Misty asked.

"Not yet. How about you?"

"I'm a free spirit. I can't imagine any man happy with me traveling around the country for these wedding fairs. Who would be at home to darn his socks and make sure his dinner was on the table in time?" She laughed. "Maybe that's unfair on our hairier counterparts. I'm all for finding love, you've just got to make sure it's with the right person. Someone who'll encourage you to grow and become the best version of yourself."

We walked along, chatting about the dogs, marriage, and the castle some more. Misty was clearly as crazy about dogs as I was, and was happy to indulge Saffron and her spiky ways, not minding when she tugged on her lead or growled.

Meatball edged closer to Saffron and risked a sniff. He got barked at for his efforts.

"I don't think you'll make a new friend here," I said to him.

"Saffron, where are your manners?" Misty lifted her gently off the ground and held her in her arms. "She's probably tired. She's only a little thing but has a lot of energy. I like to walk her until she's exhausted, so it's easy to get her to sleep. Connie works long hours during the wedding fairs. When she's not looking after the display, she's creating new bouquets to put out for the next day. She works till well after midnight, so I look after Saffron during the night as well. She insists on sleeping on the pillow right next to my head."

"I occasionally sneak Meatball into bed with me," I said.

"A bed isn't as comfortable if it doesn't have a dog on it," Misty said.

My phone rang in my pocket, and I pulled it out. Alice was calling me.

"Take that if you need to," Misty said.

"Thanks. I'd better." Alice didn't like to be ignored. "Hi, Alice. I'm just out walking Meatball. Do you—"

"There's an emergency. You're needed."

"To do what?"

"We have to walk the catwalk tonight."

I wasn't sure I'd heard her right. "What are you talking about? We're going to see the models walk the catwalk in a couple of hours."

"No! The models are all sick. I snuck backstage to take a look at the dresses before the event started. There are only three models left standing. They can't show all the dresses they want to. So I volunteered us."

I tipped back my head and groaned. "Alice, no! I'm not made for the catwalk. I'm made for the dog walk only."

"Please. It'll be so much fun. They're not expecting us to be professional models."

"I'm not an anything model. I'm not made for strutting around in a long dress and showing off in front of strangers."

"I am, and I insist we do it. It'll be fun. And I've convinced Rupert to take part. The organizers are almost fainting with delight. And it's drawing quite a crowd. Apparently, they put out something on social media that a princess will be walking for them in their showcase wedding gown. Imagine that."

I gritted my teeth. "I am. It's horrifying."

"That's not nice. I'll look amazing."

"You will. You'll be the star of the show. But I'll look ridiculous. Dresses don't suit me."

"They do. You scrub up well. You have to do this with me. I need you by my side."

"I'm happy to watch from the sidelines and cheer you on, but I can't wear a wedding gown. It really isn't me."

Misty touched my arm. "I've been to plenty of these catwalk shows. The models they use aren't your usual supermodel types. They come in all shapes and sizes to represent the different brides. I think you'll be perfect."

I wrinkled my nose. I wasn't convinced.

"How about you take Meatball with you on the catwalk as well?" Misty said. "He looks like a confident dog. He'll enjoy strutting along the catwalk in a smart bow tie."

"Who are you with?" Alice asked.

"I met Saffron and her walker, Misty. We were taking a stroll in the woods."

"I heard what she said. You have to listen to her," Alice said. "Besides, I've already said we'll do it. You can't let everybody down."

I grumbled under my breath. Alice always landed me in situations like this. "One dress."

"Seven dresses," Alice said.

"That's way too much lace and silk for me. Two dresses."

"Seven dresses," Alice said. "Just pretend you're playing dress up like you did when you were a child."

"I didn't play dress up. I liked mud pies. Can't I just help you change outfits? And maybe Lady Diana could be a model."

"She point-blank refused and shut herself in her bedroom. She's being an absolute misery again and keeps complaining of a stomach ache. She said she'd walk down the catwalk in tears if I made her do it. That's hardly going to sell wedding dresses or give Audley Castle a good reputation. I gave up on her. Please, you're my only hope."

"You should do it," Misty said. "The catwalks are fun. You get a free makeover and they serve champagne to ease the nerves."

"I'll need a bucket of champagne to get through this."

Misty chuckled. "I'll be there with Saffron to applaud you."

I looked down at Meatball, who stood patiently by my side. "What do you think? Are we brave enough to go on a catwalk?"

He wagged his tail and double woofed.

I puffed out a breath. "Okay, we'll do it."

"Excellent," Alice said. "I'll find something cute for Meatball to wear. I'm sure there were a couple of stalls selling wedding outfits for dogs."

"Just a neck tie of some sort. We don't want him ripping off his tuxedo mid-walk and exposing himself to the blushing brides."

Alice roared a laugh down the phone. "That would be hilarious."

We finished our conversation, and I stuffed my phone back in my pocket.

Misty grinned at me as we continued to walk along the path. "I promise you, the catwalks are fun. I've seen plenty of them in my time working the wedding fairs. Just treat it like a party and don't get stressed. The women are here looking at the dresses, not you. And you've got a lovely figure. You're perfect for some of the designs."

"Do any of them come with a mask so no one will see my face?"

She chuckled. "No masks. But the makeover will make you look beautiful. Not that you need much makeup to do that."

"Thanks. Do you know what's wrong with the models?" I said.

"Not really. Several of them left earlier today," Misty said. "I think there's some nasty bug going around. I'm glad I haven't gotten it. It's thanks to all the fresh air I get walking the dogs. It keeps me healthy. Once I've taken Saffron back and settled her in, I've got three more little ones to walk, so I get plenty of exercise."

"Let's hope the exercise keeps the bug away from me, too." I glanced over my shoulder. "I should head back to the castle. I need to get ready to be a smiling, confident bride for the evening."

"I'll come with you. Saffron is beginning to whine, which always precedes a temper tantrum." She set the dog back on the ground, and we turned and made our way toward the castle, chatting more about our dogs.

Misty was warm and friendly. Her positive mood was even rubbing off on Saffron, who'd stopped growling and snarling at Meatball. Maybe there was a friendship developing between them.

I squinted as we rounded a corner, a blue flashing light hitting my eyes.

"Oh! What's that ambulance doing outside the castle?" Misty glanced at me, alarm in her eyes.

"I don't know." I increased my pace, Meatball hurrying along beside me. "Maybe a visitor got sick."

"It's not uncommon at wedding fairs. All the excitement and stress can make people faint."

We were approaching the main entrance, when Alice raced out. She saw me and dashed over. "The most awful thing has happened."

"Is it someone in the family? Not Rupert?" I asked.

"No! He's fine. The family is fine." Alice sucked in a breath. "One of the florists at the wedding fair, Connie Barber. She's dead."

Chapter 5

"Connie's dead!" Misty's face paled as she stared at Alice. "What … what happened to her?"

"Princess Alice Audley, this is Misty Gilchrist. She was hired by Connie to look after her dog." I made a swift introduction.

Alice nodded, her hands clasped. "I'm sorry to be the bearer of such bad news. I'm not sure what's going on. Connie was found in a public restroom, curled up in one of the stalls. Fortunately, one of our cleaners found her, along with Connie's assistant. The public don't know what's going on. The paramedics are bringing Connie out in a moment."

"I thought she didn't look well when I saw her in the marquee," I said. "She had a strange tint to her skin."

"Was it a spray tan gone wrong?" Alice asked.

I shook my head. "No. And her eyes looked yellow."

"Hmmm, you don't spray tan your eyeballs," Alice said.

Misty picked up Saffron and cuddled her against her chest. "Connie did like a drink. I suggested she took things steady."

"She was an alcoholic?" Alice asked.

Misty's bottom lip wobbled. "I don't like to speak ill of the dead, but she had a problem. I suggested she take a break and get professional help, but she wouldn't listen. Connie had a stubborn streak."

"When I saw her arguing with Belinda, she seemed unsteady on her feet," I said. "Belinda even accused her of drinking too much. Was it really such a problem?"

"I blame the stress," Misty said. "Having a few drinks was Connie's way of coping with her growing business."

"I'm so sorry for your loss," Alice said to Misty.

"That's kind of you to say. She was my boss, but I considered her a friend as well. We'd often have tea and homemade cake together and talk about our day. That won't happen anymore." She snuggled a sleepy looking Saffron closer. "You sweet baby. You've just lost your mom."

Saffron didn't seem remotely bothered as she licked Misty's chin.

"Connie couldn't have been much older than me," Alice said.

"She was in her early thirties," Misty said. "Far too young to die. I'd better go and find out what's going on." She nodded at me before hurrying away with Saffron.

"You're sure this was an accident?" I asked Alice.

She blinked at me. "I didn't see the body, but everyone's talking about it. If Connie had a problem with drink, maybe she overdid it. We can't worry about that now. We have a catwalk to get ready for."

I stared at the ambulance. It was hard to believe that someone I'd spoken to so recently was dead.

"Holly! Stop being so nosy. Let's move. We have wedding gowns to try on. We need to make sure they fit before we take to the catwalk. And your hair needs attention."

"My hair is just fine." I smoothed a hand over my windswept hair.

"It is if you like the wild woman look. No stalling. It's time we were made into beautiful brides."

I let Alice drag me and Meatball into a large white marquee and over to the back section that had been curtained off. Several people were setting out chairs along a long catwalk that was being erected.

My stomach flipped over and nerves fluttered inside me. Was I really brave enough to do this?

"This will be such fun." Alice bounced on her toes. "The dresses are divine."

I nodded. "Who found Connie in the bathroom? You said it was a cleaner and Connie's assistant?"

"That's right. It was Betsy Malone," Alice said. "She was quite overcome, as you can imagine, stumbling over a dead body like that. It's a good job the girl with the pink hair was there to keep her upright, or two people would be going to hospital. Well, one to the morgue and the other to a ward because she fainted. Poor Betsy. Such a shock for her."

I arched an eyebrow. Stumbling over a body had happened to me once or twice. It never got any easier. "How's Betsy doing?"

"I had to give her a large brandy to calm her nerves."

I sighed. I liked Betsy, but she was a terrible gossip. This news would be all over the village before the end of the day. "Did she see anything unusual about the body?"

Alice shot me an irritated glance. "Not everyone who dies in the castle is murdered. You have such a suspicious nature."

"I don't! I just want to make sure nothing bad happened to Connie. She seemed to be having a few struggles and wasn't happy."

"She was sick, drinking too much, and it caught up with her. Let's go and have a look at the gowns. I get first pick."

"Connie must have drunk a lot for it to kill her." I turned, my gaze on the exit. I should go back and check things out.

Alice pulled out an off the shoulder white gown with a mermaid tail and held it out in front of me, stopping me from going anywhere.

"Have you spoken to Campbell about what happened to Connie?" I asked.

"Holly! It's not a security matter. An alcoholic died from drinking too much at a wedding fair. The sooner the tragic tale is forgotten about the better. What do you think about this gown?"

"Alice! That's ruthless. A woman is dead."

She lowered the gown and scowled at me. "I've had enough misery and bad news having to look after Diana these past few days. I want fun. Of course, I'm sorry Connie is dead, but there's nothing I can do to change that. And we're both alive and about to have a fab evening, but only if you stop dwelling on dead people."

"Are you sure the catwalk should even happen?"

"Yes! I'm absolutely sure. Don't make Connie's death a reason you can't take part. I know you're worried about showing yourself to the crowd. You'll soon get over your nerves."

"I'd never be so calculating." I'd thought about using this death as a reason not to be involved for a brief second.

"We're both models for the evening. I want a makeover, my hair done, and to wear a pretty dress or seven," Alice said. "And I want you to do it alongside me. Plus, you get to walk the catwalk with my brother."

I took a step back, bumping into a rack of gowns. "What do you mean?"

Alice turned and grinned. "I knew you'd be excited when you heard about that. You're going to pose as Rupert's bride. Isn't that hilarious?"

My heart thudded in my chest. I'd maybe had one or two fantasies about being Rupert's bride, but that's all they'd ever be. Now, I'd get the chance to do it for real? Well, for real as in on a catwalk pretending to be his bride, but it was close enough to the real thing.

Alice giggled. "Maybe it's a portent." She tipped her head back and groaned. "I'm having a vision, just like Granny. You're going to be my sister-in-law."

I smacked her on the arm. "Don't joke about that. Although I should go and speak to Lady Philippa about what happened to Connie. She could have seen something about her death."

"There's no time for that. And Granny would have summoned you if she thought anything strange was going to happen at the wedding fair. There's nothing suspicious about Connie's death. Stop trying to distract me from these gowns and get hunting for your perfect wedding dress. You need to look stunning standing next to my oaf of a brother, so no one notices when he trips over his own feet."

I shrugged off my jacket and tried to show interest in the gowns, but my thoughts were whirling. As soon as I could, I'd check in with Betsy and get the details about Connie. Maybe it really was just a tragic accident, a stressed woman weakened by illness and pushing herself too hard.

I also wanted a chat with Lady Philippa. Through her uncanny and not completely understood ability to predict deaths in Audley Castle, she should have seen this coming.

Before I could dwell on the tragic circumstances, Alice whisked me away to the changing rooms with half a dozen gowns over her arms, then I was thrust into a chair, my face covered in a thick layer of makeup, and my hair teased into curls and pinned on my head.

Meatball bounded around the changing area, getting strokes from the other models, before he returned to my side. He looked at me as if I were a stranger.

"Don't worry. All this makeup doesn't change me." I took a treat from my pocket and threw it for him.

"Isn't this fun?" Alice looked over at me from the chair she sat in.

I blinked at my reflection in the mirror. No wonder Meatball appeared startled. I looked like a different person. I rarely wore much makeup, and never the dramatic dark eyeshadow or false lashes I currently sported.

"You look really pretty," Alice said. "Rupert will have a heart attack when he sees you. He gets all silly around you when you're dressed in your apron."

Heat rose up my neck. "Rupert's always very nice to me."

"Because he's in love with you," Alice said.

I glanced around, not wanting that rumor spread by anyone. "Shush. It's not like that." I found myself getting warm and flapped a hand in front of my face.

"Ready to go in five minutes, ladies." A woman hurried past with a clipboard. "Is there anything I can get you, Princess?"

"A cold compress for my friend." Alice giggled. "And my brother. Where's Rupert?"

"I'm right here."

I hopped from my seat and smoothed my hands over the tight white bodice of the gown I wore. I turned to face Rupert, and my breath caught in my throat. He wore a striking black tuxedo suit with a white shirt underneath.

His jaw dropped and his gaze ran over me. "Holly! I almost didn't recognize you. You look …"

"She looks stunning." Alice climbed off her seat and walked over. "We both do."

She wore a fishtail gown and had several large white feathers sticking out of her blonde curls. The look wouldn't have worked on many people, but she pulled it off.

"I mean, yes, you both look magnificent. Holly, you make a striking bride."

I couldn't help but smile. "You also make a very handsome groom, Rupert."

His chest puffed out. "I do? Let's hope some lucky girl gets the opportunity to walk along the aisle with me one day."

"And it's Holly this evening." Alice stood from attaching a gold bow tie to Meatball's collar. She handed me his leash and gave me a gentle nudge. "Off you go. You're opening the show."

"Thanks for not telling me that until now." Where was that bucket of champagne when I needed it?

"You'll be great. Hold on to Rupert's arm so you don't trip over the bottom of the dress," Alice said.

Rupert held out his elbow. "Don't worry, I'll catch you if you fall."

A swirl of excitement spun through me as I headed with Rupert and Meatball to the catwalk. The loud murmuring from the other side of the curtain suggested the chairs had filled up while we were getting ready.

Rupert patted my hand. "It'll be fine. If it's any comfort, all eyes will be on me. You know what people get like around the family."

"Doesn't that make you nervous?"

"I've grown up being stared at. You get used to it, although it's never pleasant. You stick by my side and share that beautiful smile with the crowd. Everyone will be entranced by your beauty. Just like I am."

Standing beside Rupert did make me feel better, as did his charming words. We only had to wait a few seconds before the lighting and music changed.

"Ladies and gentlemen, welcome to the Audley Castle wedding fair. This evening, you'll be dazzled by an array of sparkling gowns available for purchase after the show. We also have some male models displaying a fine selection of suits and wedding attire. Remember to take a note of the details of the outfits you're interested in and then see the sellers at the end of the catwalk show."

"Ready?" Rupert whispered.

"Nope," I squeaked.

He grinned. "You'll be amazing."

"Now, may I present a very special guest model for the evening. Lord Rupert Audley, his bride, and um, Meatball!"

Rupert's arm muscles tightened as I clutched at him. It was like living in a little fantasy world. I could forget my worries and indulge in the dream that I was Rupert's bride. It was a nice dream. Rupert would make a great husband.

Before I knew it, we were gliding along the catwalk. I was dazzled by all the people taking pictures of us.

Meatball trotted along, his tail wagging as he soaked up the adoration.

Rupert leaned down until his mouth was by my ear. "I expect some of those photos will make the society pages. We'll cause quite a stir."

Some of my nerves returned. "You don't think it'll cause a scandal, being photographed together?"

He chuckled, before kissing my cheek, causing the audience to sigh and take more pictures. "What's life without a little scandal?"

"Quiet? Easy? Stress free?"

He grinned and led me to the end of the catwalk, where we had even more pictures taken while the announcer discussed our clothing, and I tried not to fidget.

"You're doing really well," Rupert whispered.

"Only six more dresses to go."

He laughed and escorted me off the catwalk, my hand tucked securely in his elbow. I needed to be careful, or I could get used to this.

We headed back into the changing area. Raised female voices had me turning, seeking out the source of the argument.

"She must have told you something." The red-haired woman I'd seen being led away by Campbell had hold of Connie's assistant, Leanna, and was shaking her.

"Get away from me. You're crazy." Leanna tried to break free, but the woman held on tight.

"You must have covered for her. She pays your wages. Tell me what you know."

"Perhaps I should intervene. I don't like to see ladies in a physical dispute." Rupert took a step forward.

"That's enough." Campbell charged into the changing room, dragged the redhead away from Leanna, and frog-marched her out.

"What was that all about?" Rupert asked. "Do you know those women?"

"Sort of. Stay here. I'm going to find out what the argument was about." I handed him Meatball's leash, hitched up the wedding dress, and raced after Campbell and the woman. In my haste, I bumped into a tall, slender woman wearing large dark glasses. "Oh! Sorry. My mistake."

The woman simply smiled and stepped out of my way.

I turned to look at her as I hurried away. Her perfume reminded me of someone.

I rounded the corner to see Campbell bundling the woman into the back of a police car, before it drove away.

He turned toward me, and his eyes narrowed a fraction. "Don't start on me. I've had enough of difficult women to last a lifetime."

"Who's that woman you just had arrested?" I asked.

"A troublemaker. Just like you." He strode past me. "By the way, nice dress."

"Thanks. You can borrow it sometime." I hurried after him. "Why have the police taken her? I saw you with her the other morning. Is she a threat to the family?"

Campbell waved me away. "Not now, Holly."

I tried to follow him, but there was no way I could keep up in this ridiculous dress and heels.

Leanna appeared outside the changing room, her face pale. "Has that awful woman gone?"

I stopped beside her. "Yes. She's with the police."

"I knew something like this would happen."

"Are you okay? Did that woman hurt you?"

She shook her head. "I'm fine. I'm almost used to her being around and causing trouble. She turns up so often."

"I'm Holly. I work at the castle. I got roped into helping tonight. Is there anything I can do to help?"

Leanna shook her head. "No, you're fine. And thanks for helping out with the catwalk event. We were stuck for models, and there was no way you'd get me doing that." She chewed on the edge of her thumbnail.

"What did you mean when you said something like this would happen?"

"Connie's death." She glanced at me and shrugged. "She had so many people who had a problem with her. I wouldn't be surprised to learn that she was murdered. And the screeching redhead should be at the top of the suspect list."

Chapter 6

I masked my surprise and did my best to keep the hem of the wedding dress from getting muddy. "Let's go back in the changing room. It's Leanna, isn't it?"

She nodded. "That's right. How do you know me?"

"I saw you at Connie's wedding stand." I waved at Alice. "How long have I got until the next catwalk?"

"Ten minutes," she said. "You'd better hurry." She stood with Rupert, his worried gaze on me.

I smiled and nodded at him to show I was fine. I rustled up two mugs of tea and sat with Leanna in a quiet corner. "I knew Connie. Well, sort of. We met a few times before she died."

Leanna grimaced. "I found her. I walked in the restroom at the same time as an older lady. We both stared at the body. Then I screamed and the other woman got a bit faint, then she went off to get help."

I sucked in a breath. "That must have been horrible."

"You got that right. It's not something I want to repeat."

"Had you known Connie long?"

"About six months. She took me on straight out of college. I want to run my own business one day. I'm hoping to get into wedding photography. Actually, I took some pictures when you were on the catwalk." Her hands shook as she took a sip of tea. "I didn't realize this business would be so cutthroat, though."

"You mean the woman who was shouting at you? She had a problem with Connie's floristry?"

"I reckon she must. I don't know much about her. Connie would never tell me who she was. She's been turning up at wedding fairs since I started working with Connie. She always tries to start a fight. I figured she was a business rival. Someone jealous of her success. Connie had a great reputation as a wedding florist. I was happy when she took me on as her assistant. I figured I'd learn loads from her."

"You also learned that the wedding business isn't all hearts and flowers?"

She snorted a quiet laugh. "It definitely isn't. Wedding planners are ruthless. There's always someone trying to undercut you or say something bad about you. And the brides! They're terrifying. Something must happen to your brain chemistry when you get asked to become someone's wife. It turns most women into monsters. Demanding, yelling, hair pulling. I saw one bride throw a vase at Connie's head because she suggested a different shade of yellow rose. Insane."

"That sounds intense."

She nodded. "It's put me right off marriage. At least, having a big wedding. When I get married, it'll be just me, my fiancé, and a few family members. No one else."

I glanced around, but no one was listening to us. "You said you wouldn't be surprised if someone killed Connie. When you discovered her body, did you see anything unusual that made you suspect her death wasn't accidental?"

Leanna placed her mug down. "I'm not sure what you're asking. I've never seen a dead body before."

"I mean, do you think the woman who was yelling at you had something to do with Connie's death? She was asking about Connie, wasn't she?"

"You're ... you're talking about murder!" The words came out on a startled squeak. Leanna grabbed her mug and gulped more tea.

I glanced around again. "What did she want to know?"

Leanna sucked in a deep breath. "I couldn't make sense of it. She kept saying I had to know about Connie's movements and who she was seeing. But I had nothing to do with Connie's diary. She handled the appointments herself. I told that woman she should have more respect for the dead, and she flew at me. Holly, do you think she killed Connie?"

I fiddled with a sequin on my wedding dress, not wanting to alarm Leanna, especially when I had no proof of foul play. "I just don't like to think of anything bad happening to Connie. And seeing how angry that woman was, and your comment, it got me wondering."

"Oh! Well, me too. And that redhead had murder in her eyes." She shuffled down in her seat. "I'm not sure what I'm going to do now she's gone. It was just the two of us running the business. Well, I assisted."

I smiled at her. "Maybe one of the other wedding florists could take you on."

"Unlikely. I've gotten to know some of the regulars who do the same wedding fairs as Connie. Behind the smiles, they're always being mean to each other. Zoe's the worst. She can be spiteful, even though she looks like an angel with all those blonde curls."

"Who's Zoe?"

"She used to work with Connie. They started Florally Forever together, but something went wrong. If I ever mentioned Zoe's name, Connie would shut me down and say she was a joke. I've seen them arguing. And then there's Belinda. She'd smile at you while sharpening a knife to stab in your back."

"I've met her. She seemed friendly enough."

"Not to Connie, or me." Leanna chewed on her thumbnail again. "So many people didn't like Connie."

I added Belinda and Zoe to my list to check out when I had a moment. "Do you know if Connie was sick before she died?"

"She's been fighting some bug for ages. I asked her about it, and she told me not to worry, but I could see she didn't look too good. And she picked up the stomach bug going around here."

"Was Connie being treated for a more serious illness? Something that could have weakened her immune system so she couldn't fight off this stomach bug."

"Oh, um, not that I know of. Like I said, she didn't talk much about her private life. She wouldn't have shared a health problem with me."

I sat back in my seat. "I heard a rumor that Connie had a bit of a drink problem."

Leanna's forehead wrinkled. "She liked a glass of champagne. And it's easily available at these fairs. I can't stand the stuff."

"The rumor wasn't true?"

She sighed. "Maybe, I don't listen to them. That's another thing I hate about wedding events. Everyone is either gossiping or getting frisky with someone they shouldn't. It's gross. You won't catch me making out with some old dude in a suit."

"Was Connie getting frisky with someone she shouldn't?"

"No one special." Leanna slumped in her seat. "I need to re-think my career. Get out before I turn into another bitter wedding planner. I didn't think it would be like this."

"I hope you sort something out," I said. "Are you staying for the rest of the wedding fair?"

"Yes. I'm not sure whether to keep Connie's display up, though. Customers who've placed orders will need to know what's happened to her. They'll have to find a new florist."

"Stay until the end of the wedding fair if you can. Maybe you can pick up some new work if you do." Plus, I wanted to keep Leanna around. She had insider knowledge on Connie's business dealings, and they didn't all sound positive.

"Holly, what are you doing? You should be getting changed into your next dress. And I thought you were going to watch me on the catwalk. I was outstanding." Alice's gaze settled on Leanna.

"Sorry. I got sidetracked. I bet you were amazing." I gestured at Leanna. "This is Leanna. She worked with Connie."

"Very nice to meet you. Now, what's this about a fight? Rupert said there was a problem when you came off the catwalk," Alice said. "Who was fighting?"

"That's what I was trying to find out from Leanna. Campbell dealt with it," I said.

Alice nodded. "Of course he did. Now, come on, we've got more wedding dresses to show off."

I'd been so focused on what was going on backstage that I'd forgotten my role as a bridal model. I turned back to Leanna. "I'd better get on. Try not to worry about that woman coming back. Now castle security has dealt with her, she won't be a problem."

"I'll be glad to never see her again," Leanna said. "Thanks for the chat. And enjoy the rest of the catwalk show. I'll try to get some more pictures of you if I get the chance."

"Thanks." I headed off with Alice, and we got changed into our next wedding gowns.

"What are you up to?" Alice asked as she shimmied into a satin dress covered in sparkling crystals.

"Something strange is going on."

"You're still thinking about what happened to Connie?" Alice turned so I could button up the back of her dress.

"Not many people liked her. Leanna told me that the woman who was taken away by Campbell threatened her."

"Why would she do that?"

"That's what I need to find out. What did Connie do that was so bad?"

"There's one person who'll have the answer to that," Alice said. "Let's finish up here and find Campbell."

"He won't tell us anything."

"He'll tell me everything. I'll insist he does." She fluttered her eyelashes. "He can never resist me."

"More like, he can never resist knowing he'll get paid at the end of the month."

She poked out her tongue. "Don't be mean."

I adjusted the veil on my head. "You're a braver woman than I am to demand answers from Campbell."

"I'm not brave. I'm simply prettier, richer, and more influential."

"And a thousand times less modest."

She giggled. "You make a glorious bride-to-be. Let's go wow the crowd."

An hour later, I'd walked up and down the catwalk in all the dresses, and was relieved to peel myself out of the last one and put on my normal clothes. Being a model was exhausting, and my face hurt from having to fake a smile for such a long time.

"I've summoned Campbell." Alice met me outside the changing rooms. "He's on his way."

"He'll be in a terrible mood."

"He's always pleasant around me. I'll do the talking. He does tend to get moody when you question him."

I was happy to let Alice lead. Campbell had already spotted me snooping around and wasn't happy about it.

"There he is. Let's go." Alice caught hold of my arm and hurried me over to where Campbell stood outside the marquee.

"Princess Alice." He nodded at her, before his gaze cut to me. "Holmes."

"We have questions for you," Alice said. "We need an update on Connie Barber's death."

"What information do you require?" Campbell's eyes narrowed, his attention fixed on me.

"Holly thinks her death was odd. How did she die?" Alice asked.

"The exact cause of death has yet to be determined," Campbell said.

"Do you think it was murder?" I couldn't resist asking.

"As I said, it's to be determined." The muscles in Campbell's jaw flexed.

"She was very young to drop down dead," Alice said. "Could she have had a problem with her heart?"

"It's possible." Campbell's face gave nothing away.

"There's a rumor she had a drink problem," I said.

Alice turned to me, her eyebrows raised. "Really? Well, Campbell, what do you know about that?"

"I didn't know the woman. I can't confirm that either way," Campbell said.

"Has an autopsy been arranged?" I asked.

"Of course. With any unusual death that happens."

"That should sort things out," Alice said. "We'll soon know how she died. Is there anything else you need to ask, Holly?"

I detected a faint growl coming from Campbell. "Who was the woman you removed from the marquee? The one yelling at Leanna?"

"She's not relevant to Connie's death. She's a troublemaker who keeps breaking into the wedding fair."

Alice grabbed his arm. "It's just us. Surely you can tell me her name. She's not a risk to me, is she?"

Campbell's back stiffened. "Absolutely not, Princess. I'm still gathering all the facts about her, but she won't be a problem to you."

"Can I have a little clue about her?" Alice said.

"Are you certain it's you who wants this information?" Campbell arched an eyebrow and glared at me.

"You're such a tease." Alice lightly tapped his arm. "It's important I know everything that goes on in the castle."

"You'll be the first to hear when I have concrete information about her. If you'll excuse me, Princess, I need to continue with my duties."

Alice nodded. "Very well. You're dismissed."

He turned and strode away, his fingers flexing and his shoulders tight around his ears. I'd pay for that later.

"Campbell wasn't much use," Alice said. "I'm sure he was keeping information from us. I hate to be kept in the dark."

"I agree. He knows more about that woman. He just wasn't willing to share."

"I could call him back and insist he reveal everything." She sucked in a breath.

I grabbed her arm and shook my head. "Please, don't. He'll only take it out on me. You don't want your best friend to vanish and never be seen again."

Confusion crossed her face. "Of course not. But why would that happen?"

"Because Campbell thinks I lead you astray and wants to put a stop to it."

She giggled. "You absolutely do. And I wouldn't have it any other way. If your body turns up, I'll make sure

Campbell pays for it."

"How comforting. Or maybe we can just stop prodding at him, so he never disposes of me in the first place."

"Where's the fun in that?" Her smile faded. "Do you really think Connie's death was the result of foul play?"

"I'm not certain. We could benefit from some insider knowledge. I'd like to talk to Lady Philippa and see if she knows anything."

"She'd have summoned you if she predicted this death. It's what she always does."

"She could be distracted. Maybe the wedding fair has taken her eye off things."

"We can visit her tomorrow morning if you like."

"Great. She can point us in the right direction."

"Or put your concerns to bed. You may simply be seeing murder when it's nothing but a sad alcoholic who pushed her luck."

"Even so, she could give us a clue."

Alice shuddered. "I don't know how she does it. I find the whole business incredibly creepy. I like to think it's a little quirk of hers. Wouldn't it be terrible if it got passed down to me? I don't want to have visions of people dying. I want happy dreams."

"Have you ever had a premonition?"

"No. I mainly dream about being on a beach, and … someone is rubbing suntan lotion in my back." Her cheeks grew pink.

It didn't take a genius IQ to figure out who that someone was. "I'll fix us a nice breakfast, and we can go up to Lady Philippa's turret and talk murder."

"Excellent. I'll have pancakes tomorrow. You always make the best pancakes. Plenty of syrup on mine. And chocolate chips."

I curtsied. "Any more demands, your majesty?"

She giggled. "Throw in some croissants as well. Make sure they're fresh."

"My croissants are always fresh."

Alice gave me a quick hug. "How exciting. Another mystery to solve. I'll see you in the morning."

I collected Meatball and the rest of my things and headed back to my apartment, mulling over the events of this evening. Something odd was going on when it came to Connie Barber's death, and I was determined to find out what it was.

I was rummaging through my purse for my keys, when the sound of scuffling feet had me looking up.

Meatball growled, and his hackles rose.

It was dark by my apartment. The new moon overhead cast barely any light.

I clenched my keys between my fingers, my heart pounding. Was it Connie's killer, back to take another victim?

Staring into the gloom, I swallowed down my fear as someone moved in the shadows. "I can see you. Come out. Why are you hiding?"

There was a soft feminine chuckle, and a woman stepped out from behind a bush. "You were always too good at hide and go seek. Hello, Holly. It's been a while."

I stared at her, not able to believe what I was seeing. "Oh my goodness! Granny Molly."

Chapter 7

"Are you going to stand there and stare or give your old gran a hug?" Granny Molly held her arms open.

I stumbled into her embrace and gripped her tightly. "How are you here?" She smelled the same as always, jasmine perfume and hairspray.

"Let me into your apartment, and I'll tell you everything." She squeezed me hard before stepping back, her bright eyed gaze running over me. "You're looking well."

"You, too." Her hair was sleek and styled around her angular face. She had a few lines around her eyes, but she was still an attractive woman, with a wide mouth and a ready smile.

"Prison life suits some people." She patted me on the arm.

I had so many questions that I didn't know where to start. I fumbled the key into the lock and opened the door.

Meatball whined and lifted a paw, his head cocked as he studied the new arrival.

"This is Meatball," I said. "Do you remember him?"

"Of course. I know all about him from your letters." Granny Molly knelt and held a hand out. "You've made quite an impression on my granddaughter."

Meatball thoroughly sniffed her fingers. He wagged his tail, seeming happy to have her around. So was I, but I was shocked to the core that she was here.

I flicked on the lights and took off my jacket. I headed into the kitchen, Granny Molly following me, taking a moment to calm my racing pulse.

I turned to her. "Okay, I need to start with the most important question. Are you supposed to be out of prison?"

Her warm, loud laugh had me smiling. I'd missed that sound.

"Of course. What do you think, I made a jailbreak and am on the run?"

I tilted my head from side to side. "Well, anything's possible when it comes to you."

"Less of your cheek. Put that kettle on, make me a strong mug of coffee, and I'll tell you everything." Granny Molly took a moment to look around the kitchen. "Nice setup you've got here."

I filled the kettle and switched it on. "It comes with the job."

"That's right. I remember. I was so proud when I heard you got a job working in a fancy castle," Granny Molly said. "You're still enjoying it?"

"Very much. I love it here." My smile faded. "You could have told me you were coming."

"I wanted to surprise you. I spoke to your step-mom when I got out and thought it was time I caught up with you. I wanted to see how you were doing."

"I bet Valerie was surprised to hear from you."

"She looked almost as shocked as you. I even spoke to Bianca."

My nose wrinkled. I had almost nothing in common with my step-sister. "And how's she doing?"

"Ha! She sputtered a few words at me and then pretended there was someone at the door. She couldn't get away fast enough."

I sighed. Families were complicated.

"Anyway, I'm here to find out about you. Is everything good?"

"Yes, really good. How long have you been out?"

"A month."

"You waited all that time before coming to see me?"

She grinned. "Don't fret. I hadn't forgotten you. I've been busy. I needed to find a place to live and earn a living."

I made her a coffee and handed it to her. "What are you doing for work?"

She arched a thin eyebrow. "Do you really want to know that answer?"

I grabbed a tin of cookies, and we headed into the lounge and settled on the couch. "Is it illegal?"

"There's not much work to be had for someone who's been in prison," Granny Molly said, a defiant tilt to her chin. "I do what I need to do to get by."

"Gran! You're supposed to be a reformed character."

"I am. I even got my bookkeeping qualification while I was inside. How's that for a respectable citizen?"

"That's great. Can't you get a job doing that?"

She laughed again. "If only everyone was as open-hearted as you. If they were, I'd be in charge of the Bank of England. But as soon as people learn I have a criminal record, they don't want to know. Don't you worry about me, I'm doing fine."

"Does your new money making venture have anything to do with you coming here?" As much as I loved my gran, she was always looking for an angle, a way to get something out of a situation.

She patted my hand. "There's nothing you need to worry about. Whatever I do, it won't trace back to you."

That wasn't reassuring. "The Audley family has been great to me."

"And you think I've come to cause trouble for them?" She shook her head, hurt flashing in her eyes for a second before it vanished. "I haven't been anywhere near the family. I haven't even taken a peek inside the castle. I've been mainly watching you. Seeing you work. You made quite the pretty picture on the catwalk with that posh lord by your side."

"Oh!" I jerked upright in my seat. "That was you! You were there in the marquee. I walked into you."

"More like you almost knocked me off my feet chasing after that big scary guy. What was all that about?"

"That big scary guy is the castle's head of security, Campbell Milligan. You need to stay as far away from him as possible."

"He doesn't worry me. I've met his type before. All muscle and mouth and not a brain cell to be had."

"Please, don't tangle with Campbell. He can be mean."

"I'll stay out of his way. But what did that woman do to him? The one he put in the police car."

I let out a sigh and rubbed my forehead. "I'm not completely sure. She could be involved in another woman's death."

Granny Molly's eyes widened. "Tell me everything."

I gave her a quick update about Connie's death and my suspicions. "When I was at the bridal show, I got talking to Connie's assistant, Leanna. She revealed there weren't many people who liked Connie."

"And you think one of them did something to her and left her for dead in the toilet?"

"I haven't got any proof. At least, not yet. But Connie was surrounded by people who didn't like her. I just need to be sure she wasn't murdered. An autopsy is being done, so the police must also have their suspicions."

"When a young woman drops down dead, they're going to take a closer look. That doesn't mean this was murder." Granny Molly grinned. "You always loved a mystery when you were younger. Do you remember, I used to read you those books where the group of children went out and solved mysteries?"

"Of course. I made you read me those stories over and over again until the spines broke." I'd loved having her around when I was a kid. She was always so much fun. And always happy to invent worlds with me and solve puzzles.

"I guess some of that must have rubbed off," Granny Molly said. "You're still chasing mysteries."

"One or two," I said. "The castle brings a lot of interesting people to it."

"A lot of rich ones as well, I imagine."

I shook my head. "Don't even go there. This is my home, and it's where I work. Please don't cause any trouble."

"Holly, I'm ashamed of you. As if I'd do such a thing. I simply came here to see my favorite granddaughter."

"Your only granddaughter."

She laughed. "It's the same thing. Anyway, I came here to see you."

Guilt tickled at me for thinking the worst. "You really came here just for me?"

She grabbed a cookie and bit it in half. "These are really good. Did you make them?"

"Yes. Don't avoid the question."

She set her mug down. "Things have been tricky since I got out. I'm having a tough time. I did come here to see you, but when I saw all those well-heeled types strutting around and flashing the cash, I couldn't resist."

I groaned. "Don't tell me you've been picking people's pockets?"

"Only the rich ones. They won't miss a few bits. You know I only take from the wealthy. I'm a modern day Robin Hood."

"Granny! You're a modern day nightmare. You have to stop. And you have to return what you've taken."

"It's too late for that. Those people are long gone."

"Hand their things into the police. You could always say you found them."

"They'd take one look at my record and know it was me," she said.

My initial joy at seeing her faded. As much as I loved my gran, I couldn't have her around, not if she was going to steal.

"I've seen that disapproving look before," she said as she went to stand. "Maybe it's best if I go."

Despite my concerns, I didn't want her to leave. I'd missed not having her around. "Where are you staying?"

"I haven't decided yet. I'll figure something out."

"It's getting late. Stay here tonight. We can sort something out in the morning." And if she was under my roof, she couldn't get in any more trouble.

She reached over and hugged me. "You're such a good girl. And while I'm here, maybe I can help you with this mystery."

"It's best you don't get involved. You need to keep a low profile, and definitely no more lifting purses."

"I can do that. Although I may already have something to help you with your mystery. Are you interested in learning who got taken away by the police tonight?"

"Of course. I tried to find out who she was from Campbell, but he was tight-lipped, as usual. Do you know her?"

"Not as such. But I may have lifted her purse."

I squeezed my eyes shut. "I'll pretend you didn't tell me that."

Granny Molly chuckled. "Don't you want to find out all about her? It could help solve your mystery."

I opened my eyes and sighed. "You could have stolen a killer's purse."

"I know. I'm a terrible person, but this could help. Why don't we take a quick peek and see what secrets she has?"

Despite feeling conflicted, I really did want to know all about this woman. Granny's thieving was wrong, but maybe this was a way to make amends, by helping me figure out this puzzle.

"Go on. Let's take a look," I said.

Granny opened her large shoulder bag, rifled around, and pulled out a red leather purse. "This one is hers. She left her bag unattended while skulking around the changing rooms. It's her own fault her purse was taken."

"Let's not comment on that, shall we?"

She grinned and opened the purse. "Here we are. Her name is Tina Kennon."

I looked at the driver's license she handed me. "She's not from around here. Anything else in the purse?"

She pulled out a few more cards and a slip of paper. "There's a reservation here for a hotel. The Walden Inn."

"That's a small bed-and-breakfast on the edge of the village. She must be staying there."

"There you go. Useful information. You can head over there and find out all about her. I could always come with you."

"Not right now. And Tina's most likely still with the police," I said. "With a bit of luck, they'll deal with her, especially if she had anything to do with what happened to Connie."

"You're really worried about this Connie," Granny Molly said. "I see it in your eyes."

I shrugged. "I don't know how to explain it. I just feel that something isn't right."

"Have you felt gassy lately?"

"What? Gran! Why ask that?"

She laughed. "I'm the same. Sometimes, my stomach won't settle. I know then that something is wrong. We're the same. You should follow your gut."

"Maybe I just ate a bad salad." I pressed a hand on my stomach. Despite my protest, I did find that following my instinct often took me in the right direction.

"You make sure nothing bad happened to Connie. I may not always tread on the right side of the law, but I won't stand for murder. That's wrong," Granny Molly said.

I nodded. "I just hope the police can figure out what happened to her." I stared at the reservation slip.

"If they can't, I'm certain you will. You always were the cleverest in this family. Even when you were a youngster, I saw it in you."

"Unfortunately, that's gotten me in more trouble than I care to remember, especially since I started working at Audley Castle."

"You! In trouble. I want to know everything." She clasped my hand, a big smile on her face.

I couldn't help but grin in return. My granny wasn't the most honest of women, but she was always upfront, full of love, and would share her last slice of bread if she saw someone in need.

I curled up on the couch and told her some of the fun and games I'd had since starting work at the castle.

Tomorrow, I'd figure out what happened to Connie, then things could go back to normal. Although I wasn't certain how normal things would be with Granny Molly in the village.

Chapter 8

"Have you got everything you need?" I stood by the front door of my apartment with Meatball by my side.

My gran was tucking into a large bowl of granola with a side order of vanilla pancakes I'd made her. "Don't worry about me. I'll keep myself entertained."

"Stay in the apartment today. If castle security figure out what you've been up to, they won't hesitate in arresting you." I was in two minds whether to tell them what my granny had been doing. It was wrong, but I loved her and didn't want to see her back in prison.

She waved her spoon at me. "I'll behave myself. You get to work. I don't want you getting in trouble because of me."

It was a bit late for that. I said a quick goodbye and hurried out of the apartment with Meatball. I was leaving earlier than usual. I had two tasks on my list this morning before I started in the kitchen. First off, there was a speedy trip to the Walden Inn to see what I could find out about Tina. Dolores, the owner, was always happy to talk if I supplied the cake. Then, I was seeing Lady Philippa and Alice for breakfast.

"We don't have time to cycle this morning. Wait here, Meatball. We need to use a van." I headed into the kitchen, grabbed the keys from the locker, along with a fresh batch of blueberry blast muffins, scribbled a note to say I had the van keys, and then hurried out. "Let's go."

Meatball bounded along with me, happy to be out on an early morning adventure.

I pulled out of the castle driveway and made the ten minute journey to the Walden Inn. It was a beautiful Tudor detached house with blackened beams running across the outside and a sparkling whitewash. Dolores Wildman lived there and opened up a few rooms during the busy tourist season to accommodate visitors.

I was about to climb out of the van, when I froze. An ominous and familiar looming shape strode out the front door of the inn.

I ducked in my seat. "Meatball, hide! If Campbell sees us here, he'll be furious."

Meatball dropped on his belly and covered his head with a paw.

I shuffled as low down in the seat as I could, just keeping my eyes above the steering wheel.

Campbell didn't look my way as he marched to the large black SUV parked outside the inn. He climbed in and drove away.

I blew out a breath as I sat upright. "He must be gathering information about Tina. Let's see what he discovered."

I clipped on Meatball's leash, and we headed to the inn. Inside was a large, warmly lit entrance hall with framed photographs of the surrounding countryside on the walls. A small desk sat to one side where visitors could sign in and out and leave their keys when they were checking out if no one was around.

Dolores was just heading toward the dining room. She turned when I closed the door and smiled at me.

"Holly! And Meatball. Long time no see. How's everything with you?" She walked over and petted Meatball's head.

"Great, thanks. I've got something that I think belongs to a guest." I pulled Tina's stolen purse from my bag and held it out. "Tina Kennon."

Dolores's eyebrows shot up. "What a coincidence. I just had Campbell barking at me about her. Apparently, she's in some kind of trouble."

"I heard the same. She must have … dropped her purse at the wedding fair." It didn't feel great covering for my gran, but it was either that or send her back to prison.

Dolores took the purse. "Thanks. I'll make sure to put it in her room with a note. I'll let her know you returned it."

"Oh, no, there's no need for that. I just wanted to make sure it got back to the right person."

"That's decent of you." She turned the purse over in her hands. "Although from what Campbell was saying, it sounds like Tina may not come back."

"Oh! What did he say?" I lifted the box of blueberry blast muffins.

She flashed me a smile. "We'll have to make it quick. My guests will be down soon for breakfast. This way. I'll make coffee."

"Are you busy? I imagine you've got people staying for the wedding fair." I followed her into the kitchen.

"Fully booked. Have been for weeks. Take a seat." She gestured to the large oak table in the center of the kitchen. I settled in a seat, Meatball by my feet.

"I suppose if you're so busy, you didn't notice Tina coming and going."

She set mugs in front of us and settled in her own seat before pouring out the coffee. "I always keep a close eye on my guests to make sure I meet their needs. I especially did with that one. The highly strung guests always need special attention."

"Tina was causing problems?"

"She was fine until she got drunk in the residents' bar the other evening. Then she started ranting about lies and deceit and not being able to trust anybody."

"Did she say who deceived her?" I passed over a muffin.

Dolores shook her head. She peeled back the muffin wrapper and took a bite. "Delicious, as always. I kept well away from Tina. I just made sure she wasn't causing a problem for the other guests. But after she'd had her fifth large gin, I gently suggested she go to bed and sleep it off."

"And did she?"

"After some protesting." Dolores leaned closer. "I'm glad she's no longer here. I'm hoping she won't come back. When her room was cleaned this morning, the maid found some unsettling pictures."

"Of what?"

Dolores took another bite of muffin. "A woman with her eyes scratched out."

I was certain I knew who that woman would be. "Did Campbell say who she was?"

"I already knew who she was. One of the pictures was taken from a newspaper. It had her name printed underneath. It's the woman who died at the wedding fair. Connie something or other."

"Barber. Do you still have the pictures?"

"Campbell took them away. And he gave nothing away when I asked him what was going on, but it sounds suspicious." She finished her muffin. "What's Tina got to do with Connie's death? I heard she was alone when she died."

I sipped my coffee. "The news is already around the village?"

Dolores gave me a warm smile and a gentle shrug. "You know Audley St. Mary, we love our gossip. I've heard several versions of how she died, but she was alone each time, which doesn't suggest anything odd happening. What do you know about her?"

"Not much. I met her a couple of times at the wedding fair."

"And?"

I tilted my head. "And what?"

"Holly! You always have opinions about the strange goings on at the castle. People often talk about it."

"I do?" I drank more coffee. "What do people say about me?"

She laughed and patted my hand. "Nothing bad. And everyone raves about your baking. They also talk about how helpful you are when it comes to dealing with certain sticky situations, especially murder."

"Oh! I … I didn't know that." I looked at Meatball, broke off a piece of muffin, and fed it to him. "Is that a problem?"

"Not as far as I can see. You helping to keep the village safe makes you an asset. Now, wipe that worried look off your face and pass me another muffin."

I relaxed a little and handed over another treat. "I do think it's strange the way Connie died."

Dolores chuckled and nodded. "There you go. I heard she was found clutching a big bottle of whiskey, curled around the empty bottle in the toilet."

"Almost. I don't know about the whiskey. She didn't seem well before she died."

"And now Campbell's poking around and asking questions about Tina. Did she have something to do with it?"

"You know what Campbell's like. He plays his cards close to his chest."

"He welds them to his chest, so no one knows what he's doing. There's mysterious and then there's downright annoying."

I grinned. "That's very true."

"The way he's asking around about Tina suggests something serious happened." She sat back in her seat, the second muffin gone. "The ladies at the knitting club will be fascinated by this. Not that I gossip, of course. I'm just sharing useful information."

"Sharing information is a good thing." I hid a grin behind my mug and drank more coffee.

She flashed me a smile. "Thanks for making the trip over to bring back Tina's purse. But if she had something to do with what happened to Connie, I doubt she'll need it for a long time."

I finished my coffee. "No problem. I'd better get back. I need to get to work."

"Of course. And I've got the breakfast things to deal with. I can hear one of my guests coming down the stairs. I hope you help Campbell figure out what happened with Connie."

"I wouldn't dream of getting in his way and telling him how to do his job."

"Of course you wouldn't. Mind your step with him, or you may get flattened." Dolores led me to the front door, petted Meatball one last time, and we headed outside.

I settled in the van and looked at Meatball. "This is looking more and more like it was a murder. Let's get back to Alice and Lady Philippa and see what they think."

Chapter 9

Once I was back at the castle, I dashed into the kitchen, grabbed a selection of freshly baked croissants, scones, muffins, and pancakes, as ordered by Alice, and skipped out again before Chef Heston caught me.

"Woof, woof!" Meatball charged ahead of me, sniffing the air as he caught a whiff of the breakfast items.

In the distance, I spotted Misty walking three small dogs on leashes. I adjusted my grip on the basket and hurried to catch up with her.

Meatball was way ahead of me. He bounced around the three dogs, wagging his tail as he sniffed noses and butts.

"Hi, Misty," I said. "No Saffron with you today?"

"She won't tolerate being around these three, even though they're good-natured. She can be such a brat. I'll walk her after I've taken this lot out." Her eyes looked red-rimmed, as if she hadn't had a good night of sleep.

"What are you going to do with Saffron?" I fell into step with her as we walked along the path with the dogs.

"I haven't decided. Connie had no immediate family that I know of. She was an only child and her parents aren't alive. There's no one obvious to give Saffron to. I definitely don't want to put her in the pound."

"She'd hate that. She's used to living in the lap of luxury."

"I'm considering keeping her. When she gets over her temper tantrums, she can be sweet. Maybe life on the wedding fair circuit didn't suit her. I can't offer Saffron much in the way of fine food or fancy clothes, but she'd have a good life with me. And I'll make sure she's properly trained, so she doesn't keep snapping at other dogs."

"That sounds like a good compromise. Saffron must be as unhappy as everyone else about what happened to Connie."

"Most likely. She keeps whining and looking around. She seems confused. I hope she doesn't miss Connie too much."

"You knew Connie well, didn't you?" I said.

"I saw her every day while working for her. Connie usually took a break from the shows over the winter, but otherwise, she'd be on the road most of the time. She'd always ask me to look after Saffron."

"Did she ever tell you about any concerns she had?"

Misty glanced at me. "Concerns about anything in particular?"

"Maybe someone was threatening her business, or wanted to damage her reputation?"

Misty gave a soft chuckle. "I see you're getting to know the wedding business a little better. Behind the confetti and sugar sweet cakes are ruthless business minds. There's a lot of money to be made in arranging an extravagant wedding, and these ladies don't pull their punches when it comes to clinching a business deal. They stamp on anyone who gets in their way."

"Which suggests Connie may have made a few enemies along the way."

"More than a few. They're friendly to each other when they're at the fairs, but behind-the-scenes, it's different."

"Was there anyone in particular who had a problem with her?"

"Connie always complained about Belinda Adler. They didn't like each other. When she got started in the business, Belinda was a mentor to Connie. When Connie figured out she couldn't learn anything more from her, she dumped her. Completely abandoned their friendship. And when Belinda asked for Connie's help when she was getting divorced, Connie turned her back on her."

"Ouch! I didn't know Belinda was divorced."

Misty lifted a shoulder. "It's sort of ironic. She's promoting weddings, yet she hates them."

"She did say she was thinking of a career change. That could be why."

"Most likely. Belinda's promoting something she doesn't believe in." Misty glanced at me again. "Why are you interested in Connie's enemies?"

"I'm … doing research into wedding planners. Trying to find the right one. I don't want anyone who likes to argue or cause problems."

"For yourself? You're getting married?" Misty grinned. "I heard you caused a stir at the catwalk event by walking with a member of the Audley family."

A flush of heat spread up my neck and onto my cheeks. "I didn't have a choice. Princess Alice forced my hand. She can be very persuasive when she wants something."

"There are already pictures online. You looked beautiful in that dress. I take it you're not getting married to Lord Rupert Audley?"

"You guessed right." Not that I hadn't thought about how nice that would be once or twice.

"You made a handsome pair, if you don't mind me saying," Misty said.

I didn't want to think about that. "It was just for the show. I'd better get going. I've got breakfast to deliver. If you have any problems with Saffron and can't keep her, let me know. I know a couple of great local animal shelters. I'm sure they'll take her in if they have the room."

She looked down at the dogs she was walking. "Thanks. I'll give it some thought."

I hurried off with Meatball and headed into the east turret where Lady Philippa had her rooms. As usual, the stone staircase was a good ten degrees cooler than anywhere else.

Meatball raced up the stairs, his little claws scrabbling on the stone as he dashed past the cold spots and eerie whispers that always followed me in this part of the castle.

We arrived at Lady Philippa's door without incident, no ghosts lurking in the shadows this time, and I knocked.

"Come in if you have a basket of goodies. We're starving in here," Alice called from the other side of the door.

I pushed it open and smiled. Lady Philippa and Alice sat at the table, an expectant look on their faces. "Am I late?"

"Ten minutes!" Alice tapped her watch. "What kept you?"

"Sorry. I had an early appointment. And then I saw Misty out for a walk with the dogs." I hurried over and set out the contents of the hamper. "Misty is thinking about keeping Saffron."

"Who's Saffron?" Lady Philippa was already munching her way through an almond croissant.

"Connie's dog," I said.

"Ah! The dead woman. Alice has filled me in on the events at the wedding fair," Lady Philippa said. "Such a scandal."

I settled in a seat and selected a blueberry muffin. "You didn't predict her death?"

"No, I missed this one. I read through several of my notebooks in case I missed something while we were waiting for you to arrive. Sometimes my premonitions aren't clear and I get muddled with what they're telling me."

"Maybe you're no longer having your strange premonitions," Alice said. "That's no bad thing if they're gone. They are a bit creepy." She leaned down and fed Meatball a piece of pancake.

"My gift is important," Lady Philippa said. "It helps people."

"Not true. Everyone dies when you think about them," Alice said. "That's hardly helpful."

"Daft girl, you've got it the wrong way around," Lady Philippa said. "If I think about someone, it doesn't put death on their tail. I simply have images of their upcoming death. It's not my fault if no one can prevent them. Anyway, my thoughts have been full of weddings. I keep dreaming about them."

"The wedding fair has rather taken over the castle," I said.

"It's not the fair that's bothering me. I keep having images of you getting married, Holly."

I almost choked on my muffin, while Alice clapped her hands. "Me! Who am I getting married to?"

"This is so exciting," Alice said. "Is Rupert marrying Holly in your dreams? They looked amazing at the wedding fair. I expect the society pages will be full of gossip about who Rupert's beautiful bride is."

"I hope you set them straight if they ask any questions," I said. "I don't want the paparazzi snooping into my life and making assumptions."

"You'll be old news tomorrow. But you looked stunning in that dress. I could buy it for you so you have it when you finally get married," Alice said.

"I don't want a wedding dress," I said. My attention turned to Lady Philippa, a ball of nerves in my stomach. "Did you see who I was getting married to?"

"No, the image of the groom was fuzzy. I tried hard to see his face, but it wouldn't snap into focus. Alice is right, though, you do make a lovely bride."

"What about Alice? Any sign of her getting married soon?" I asked.

Alice shoved half a scone in her mouth and narrowed her eyes at me.

"There's no sign of a wedding for Alice," Lady Philippa said with a shake of her head.

"I don't want to get married," Alice said. "I'm happy as I am. And for now, my parents have stopped discussing marriage, so I'm off the hook. They've focused on Rupert, which is so funny. It serves him right for teasing me so much about not being able to find a man."

"You need to be careful, or you'll get the label of old maid," Lady Philippa said.

"I'm not old," Alice said. "I'm a modern independent woman who doesn't need a man by her side to feel complete. Isn't that right, Holly?"

"Absolutely." I grinned at her. I expect it would be a different story if Campbell ever got around to asking her out.

"You see! Holly doesn't want to get married, and neither do I."

"Moving on from weddings. Have none of your premonitions provided a clue about what happened to Connie?" I asked Lady Philippa. "The more I learn about her, the more I think her death was suspicious."

"I've got nothing to help you," Lady Philippa said. "But I agree, a young woman like that simply keeling over and dying does seem odd. You're looking into it?"

"Of course we are," Alice said. "We can't let this go unnoticed."

"Campbell's looking into it," I said.

"Hmmm. And we all know how well that'll turn out," Lady Philippa said. "You keep asking questions. You'll get to the bottom of this."

I swallowed my piece of scone. "Actually, that's why I was a bit late this morning. I discovered the woman who was arguing with Leanna at the catwalk show had a big problem with Connie. Her name's Tina Kennon. She's been staying at the Walden Inn. I headed over there first thing to ask around."

"What did you learn about her?" Alice asked.

"That she hated Connie. She had pictures of her in her room with her eyes scrubbed out."

"Oh, my! That's seems extreme. So, she did something bad to Connie?" Lady Philippa asked.

"Didn't you say Connie looked an odd color?" Alice said.

"She looked gray. And I'm sure the whites of her eyes were yellow tinged," I said.

"What's that a symptom of?" Alice tilted her head.

"Kidneys," Lady Philippa said. "Jaundice can turn someone yellow. Maybe she had a problem with her kidneys."

"She drank a lot," Alice said.

"We only have other people's word that she drank a lot," I said. "Although I did see her unsteady on her feet. Maybe she ignored her doctor's advice and continued to drink even though she had weak kidneys."

"The autopsy will get to the bottom of it," Alice said. "Once they've chopped her open and had a poke around inside, we'll know how she died. Then we can find out who killed her."

"You shouldn't wait for that," Lady Philippa said, her gaze on her notebooks. "You won't get the jump on the killer if you hang around and wait for the police and Campbell to catch up."

"That's what I was thinking we could do this morning," I said. "How about—"

"Oh! I knew there was something else I wanted to tell you, Holly." Lady Philippa lifted up a notebook. "I keep dreaming about a family member coming for a visit."

The scone I'd just swallowed stuck in my throat. "Really? Who's coming to see me?"

Lady Philippa tapped her finger on the notebook. "I'm not certain. I just keep seeing an older lady. And I get a knot of worry in the pit of my stomach. Do be careful around her. I'm not sure she's telling you the complete truth."

"I don't need to worry about any member of my family." My thoughts flicked to Granny Molly. Could I trust her? Maybe I shouldn't have left her in my apartment. Not that she'd take anything from me, she stuck to her rule of only stealing from those who could afford it, but what if her light fingers had bad implications for me? People were quick to assume the worst. If one family member is a bad apple, so were the rest.

"It'll be nice for Holly to have family visit," Alice said. "You're always busy working and you never take any time off."

"I'm not expecting anyone to drop by." Which was the complete truth. Granny Molly had turned up without warning.

Lady Philippa closed her notebook. "Well, my premonitions are always right."

"That's not true. You often get things muddled," Alice said. "Don't make problems for Holly when she has a murder to solve. I'm sure her family is lovely. Although it would be nice to meet some of them. You're not ashamed of us are you, Holly?"

"No! Of course not. But my family's small and often busy. And they don't live around here. Would anyone like another croissant?" I needed to get their attention off my family. I didn't want Lady Philippa predicting anything more about Granny Molly.

The croissant distraction worked, and they were soon munching on more breakfast and discussing the wedding fair.

"How about we head over to the wedding fair at lunch time?" I said to Alice. "There's someone I want to talk to. Belinda Adler has been mentioned by a couple of people. And it's pretty clear she hated Connie."

"There seem to be a lot of likely suspects in this possible murder," Lady Philippa said.

"Which is making me uneasy," I said. "Connie was surrounded by her enemies. One of them could have taken advantage and tried to make her death look accidental."

Lady Philippa nodded. "Follow your instinct. You'll figure this out."

"I can come with you to the wedding fair. I don't have anything going on this afternoon," Alice said. "Unfortunately, my morning is taken up with a piano tutorial. I'm sure I get worse after every lesson."

I grinned. "I expect your playing is better than mine. I was thinking we could suggest you're interested in finding a wedding planner. That would give us a reason to chat to Belinda about her experience and learn more about her."

Alice clapped her hands together. "Genius idea. And while we're doing that, we can find out just how much she hated Connie."

I nodded. "And if she'd do anything about it. Because if she would, she also needs to go on the suspect list."

Chapter 10

After a morning spent whipping up batches of cinnamon rolls, blueberry blast muffins, and cherry scones, I met up with Alice and we walked to the wedding fair.

We headed into one of the marquees and over to Belinda's stand. There were several people around the display, looking at the leaflets and talking to her. She was dressed impeccably in a pale blue suit, her gray bob sleek.

"I'll lead," Alice said. "After all, we're here to discuss my fake wedding."

"Are you sure you know what you're doing?"

"You question suspects all the time. It's easy." Alice cleared her throat as she approached Belinda. "I could do with some help over here."

I nudged her. "Don't go over the top. You don't want word getting out that you're actually engaged. That would make a splash in the society pages."

"At least it would get your face out of the papers," Alice said, nudging me back.

Belinda strode over, her expression morphing from shock, to surprise, and finally delight.

I stepped forward. "Hi, Belinda. May I introduce you to —"

"Princess Alice!" Belinda tripped over her feet in her haste to reach us. "It's an honor. How may I help you?"

"I hear you've been in the wedding business for a long time," Alice said. "Is there anyone I can speak to, to get a personal recommendation about your work?"

Belinda blinked hastily. "Of course. I have numerous clients who'll give me a glowing reference. Are you planning a wedding?"

"I expect I'll have to plan my own soon enough. But I'm actually interested in your business associates. I need to know that whoever I hire can work with other people and not cause any trouble. When I marry, it'll be a lavish affair. I expect to have several wedding planners. I don't want any unpleasantness."

"Oh! Well, that's unusual to have multiple planners."

"Not for the affair I intend to hold," Alice said. "Do you have anyone I may speak with?"

"Certainly. I can give you names. But I assure you, I've successfully managed extravagant weddings on my own, with no problems. I'd be delighted to look after your special day."

"You used to work with Connie, didn't you?" I asked.

Belinda's gaze ran over me, the smile on her face fading. "I did. That was a while ago."

"I'd like to talk to you about your relationship with Connie," Alice said. "I have some … concerns that need clearing up before making my decision."

Belinda's gaze hardened. "I'm not sure how that's relevant to your future wedding plans."

"It's important to me. Tell me how well you got on with Connie," Alice said.

Belinda lifted her chin. "I'm not sure what you've heard, but we had … an acceptable working relationship. I even mentored her when she was starting out."

"And you worked well together all the time?" Alice said.

Belinda's tongue poked out for a second before she licked her lips. "Unfortunately, Princess, I don't have time for this. If you're serious about hiring me, I'll send a list of people who have used my services. You'll find no complaints. I do an excellent job. I'm hard-working and efficient. I've been in the wedding business for three decades."

It looked like Belinda wasn't budging. I leaned closer. "I suggest we go somewhere quiet to talk. That is unless you want your potential clients to learn that you actually hate weddings."

Belinda blinked several times. She swallowed loudly and glanced around. "That's nonsense. This is my career. My whole life."

"But you're not happy planning weddings," I said. "We just want to learn more about Connie. I think something bad could have happened to her. You may be able to help us figure out what that was."

She shook her head. "I can't leave the stand. I may lose business."

"I'll keep an eye on things. I'm sure I can rustle up some new clients while you're away," Alice said, smiling brightly at Belinda.

"Are you sure that's a good idea?" I muttered to her. "Do you know much about weddings?"

"Unfortunately, I do. I've been to dozens of society weddings. I know exactly what clients want. I'll be able to guide them through what's expected on the big day if they have any questions. Besides, Belinda has information leaflets laid out. If I get stuck, I'll simply refer to them," Alice said.

"Um, I guess I can spare five minutes," Belinda said.

"Off you go." Alice stepped behind the display. "Welcome to Alice Audley's wedding extravaganza. I'll plan a wedding fit for a princess." She giggled.

Belinda bit her bottom lip, her worried gaze running over the display.

"Alice won't do any harm," I said. "And she's right, having a princess looking after things could be good for business. You should take advantage of her offer."

Her nose wrinkled, but she nodded. "Very well. And I could do with a cup of tea. My throat gets so dry talking to all these people."

"A chat over tea would be perfect."

She shrugged. "I'm not sure what you're expecting me to tell you about Connie."

"Let's go to the food and drink marquee. We'll find something in there, then we can talk more privately."

Belinda nodded, a glum expression on her face. She followed me out of the marquee.

"You find us seats and I'll get the tea." I hurried to the quietest looking drinks stand and paid for two teas. When I turned, it took me a minute, but I discovered Belinda sitting at the back of the marquee at a small round table. I hurried over and joined her.

She accepted the tea I gave her and took a sip. "Just so you know, I don't appreciate being coerced."

I winced. It wasn't my usual way of operating. I preferred to encourage conversation with rewards, not threats. "I wouldn't have done it if it wasn't important."

She gave a soft snort. "So, what do you want to know about Connie?"

"To start with, do you have concerns about what happened to her?"

Belinda gave me a level stare, not giving anything away. "I don't know much about it. I heard she was found in the restroom. Lots of people said there was a bottle of alcohol in her purse. Several other business owners have seen her drunk when she was working, me included. I figured she let things get out of hand."

"Did Connie have a problem with alcohol?"

"She was getting reckless, but we all like a drink at the end of a hard day. Sometimes, it feels like five o'clock can't come fast enough, especially if you've dealt with a dozen bridezillas clamoring for your attention. Maybe she was hiding a more serious drink problem. Wasn't that the cause of her death?"

"The police aren't sure. Neither am I. What was your relationship with Connie like?"

Belinda sighed. "We had our ups and downs. More downs, recently. Why do you ask?"

"Because I don't think her death was an accident."

Belinda's forehead wrinkled, and she leaned closer. "Murder?"

I nodded. "I believe so."

"Now, wait a second, is that why you're talking to me? No, absolutely not! I had nothing to do with that. We annoyed each other, but that was it. I'm not a killer." She made to stand.

I caught hold of her arm. "I'm not accusing you of anything, but have you had any recent run-ins with Connie?"

"It sounds like you are." She settled back in her seat and took a long sip of tea.

"Even though you had your problems, surely you want to know if someone killed Connie."

She let out a long sigh. "Of course. We had our spats, but no arguments spring to mind."

"Belinda, I saw you the other morning. You were fighting with Connie. And I overheard you tell her she was incompetent and needed to pull herself together. You even mentioned her drinking. Why don't you answer that question again?"

Her lips pressed together. "There doesn't seem much point, since you already know the answer. You're drawing the wrong conclusion about me, though."

"You had a problem with Connie."

She huffed out a breath. "I have a problem with a lot of people. That doesn't mean I strangle them in the toilet."

"I didn't say Connie was strangled."

"Or however it was she died. Drank too much, hit over the head, drowned, it doesn't matter, because I didn't do it." She jabbed a finger at me. "No one is talking about murder other than you. Why are you poking around in this and trying to make trouble for me?"

"Connie died in the place I live in. That's a worry. What if the killer is still on the loose?"

Belinda glanced around, her expression anxious. "No, I can't believe she was killed. It was a tragic accident."

"Did you consider her a business rival? Was she taking work away from you?"

"If she was, I didn't care. As I mentioned to you, the first time we met, I'm not happy about my choice of career."

"And I imagine, since your divorce, you may be cynical about marriage and promoting it to others?"

She jerked back in her seat. "How do you know about that?"

"People like to talk," I said.

"Well, you've got me there." She looked around again. "I don't believe in marriage, not anymore. I wish I did. I wish I could go back to a time when I was young, optimistic, and had the world in front of me. Everything seemed possible. I thought I'd found the man I'd spend the rest of my life with. I wasn't expecting it to be all moonlight and roses every day, but it got boring so quickly. My husband turned into a tedious idiot with an inability to eat with his mouth closed. I stuck with him for as long as I could, but I was miserable. Then he had the audacity to cheat on me. I gave up. So, yes, maybe I am cynical after my divorce. Can you blame me?"

"I'm sorry things didn't work out between you and your husband," I said.

"Don't be. I'm over it. And I'm over wedding fairs. I'll work one more season and then that's it. It's no longer fun."

This had me puzzled. If Belinda was giving up on the wedding industry, it gave her a weak motive. If she'd been jealous of Connie's success, I could understand her killing her, but Belinda's retirement plans sounded definite.

"At least that's something we shared," Belinda said. "For all our arguing, Connie and I were cynical about marriage. She thought it was a joke as much as I did."

"Connie had relationship problems?"

"Nothing like that. She simply said she'd never settle for one guy. She was having way too much fun being single. And why not? She was an attractive woman with plenty of disposable income. She enjoyed long weekends in Europe being wined and dined by gorgeous men. Good for her."

"There wasn't anyone special in her life?"

Belinda lifted a finger and pointed across the marquee. "Bruce Osman was always hanging around. He's like a bad smell you can't get rid of. And I always thought it was such a coincidence that he turned up at the same wedding fairs as Connie, pedaling his cheap alcohol."

"You make it sound like he was stalking her."

"It wasn't that intense. They did go out on a few dates, but Connie cooled things off. Bruce had a serious thing for her, though. He also wouldn't take no for an answer. And I've seen him get mean when he doesn't get his own way."

"Did you see him behave badly with Connie?" I studied the slick looking guy as he chatted to customers.

"They had a couple of heated arguments. Connie was a passionate woman. If anyone messed her around, she'd soon tell them to get lost. She got annoyed because Bruce was too clingy and wanted to get serious. She told him that wasn't what she was after, but he wouldn't get the hint. They had a big row, and she ended things. I don't think he ever got over her."

Could the mean former boyfriend have something to do with what happened to Connie? When I'd spoken to him, he'd been all charm and smiles, but maybe that was a front. There could be a dark side to his smoothness, something Connie experienced to her detriment.

Belinda touched the back of my hand. "I hope nothing bad happened to Connie. We had our differences, I'll admit to that, but I never wanted her dead. I miss seeing her around the wedding fair."

"Do you mind me asking where you were when Connie's body was discovered?"

Her eyebrows shot up. "You're checking my alibi?"

"Just in case. I'm trying to figure out what happened and who might have hurt her."

"I get it. If it helps you, I heard about Connie when I was ordering flowers online. There'll be a record of my purchase. And I called them as well. We spoke for about ten minutes."

I looked over at Bruce again. "Try not to worry, maybe this is just me jumping to conclusions. I do that, sometimes."

Belinda shook her head. "Now we've talked about it, it does seem strange how she died. Connie worked hard and played hard, and she had big plans for the future. She'd have hated things to end this way. She was going places.

And yes, I was envious of that, but this shouldn't have happened."

"I agree. I'll keep asking around and see what else I find out."

Belinda's eyes narrowed as she glared at Bruce. "If you discover Bruce was involved, I'll be more than happy to hunt him down for you. I never did trust that guy. All snake oil and smarm, chasing every piece of skirt who fluttered her lashes. He reminds me of my useless ex."

"Thanks for the offer. Let's hope it won't come to that." I checked the time. "You should get back to your display. Alice can get a little enthusiastic when she's excited about something. She could have sold a dozen wedding packages by now."

Belinda drained her tea and stood. "She can do what she likes with my business. I'm done with it." She nodded at me and walked away.

I sat and drank my tea, replaying our conversation. I'd had concerns about Belinda, but after speaking to her, I wasn't sure she should be on the suspect list. She appeared genuinely sad that Connie was dead, despite their differences. She was bitter and disillusioned when it came to weddings, but she didn't hold a grudge against Connie for her success, or the way she treated her.

Would I be able to get Campbell to check Belinda's alibi? I'd have to catch him in a good mood. A plate of blueberry blast muffins and Alice by my side might get him to agree to help. And if Belinda's alibi checked out, it would rule her out completely.

I shifted in my seat, my mouth watering as I took in the delicious chocolate display to my right. Maybe I had time to select a few double chocolate truffles to enjoy with my dinner.

I picked up my empty mug and stood. A sliver of unease ran down my spine. I turned, and my breath froze in my throat. Campbell was in the entrance of the marquee, glaring at me.

He beckoned me over with a finger before crossing his arms over his chest.

Whatever was about to happen, it wouldn't be good.

Chapter 11

"You've been having a productive day." Campbell peered down at me, his expression cold. "What were you talking to that woman about?"

"Nothing. Simply having a friendly chat about all things wedding related. I love a good wedding." I gave him my most innocent smile.

"And why is Princess Alice working on a wedding planning stand? Is it a coincidence that you were speaking to that woman while she's doing that?"

"Most likely. These things happen." I tried to step around him, but he blocked my path with his enormous bulk.

"I'm not buying that. What are you up to?"

I shuffled my feet and gazed at the ground. "I'm worried."

"About?"

"Connie Barber's death. If I ask you questions about her, will you answer them?"

"It's unlikely. What are your concerns?"

"I'm concerned about the way she died. It's strange. She was unwell before her death. I noticed her clutching her

93

stomach, and she had a strange tint to her skin. Have the autopsy results come back?"

"They have. I had it bumped to the top of the queue, given the sensitive nature of the death. We don't want this affecting the family."

"And? Has anything suspicious shown up? Was Connie murdered?"

His nose twitched. "You haven't told me why you were talking to Belinda."

"I won't, either, unless you answer at least one of my questions. What did the autopsy show?"

"Not here." He caught hold of my arm and hurried me out of the marquee and around the side, away from the visitors.

A tickle of nervous excitement filled my stomach. "Something showed up, didn't it? I knew it! How did Connie die?"

He grumbled under his breath for several seconds. "Her death is now considered suspicious. Connie had a high level of toxins in her system."

"It was alcohol poisoning?"

"No."

"Poison, poison! Like arsenic?"

"Keep your voice down." Campbell looked around. "It wasn't your standard poison. We believe this was a plant-based toxin. The lab is still running tests."

"Connie worked with plants every day. She'd have known if she was handling anything poisonous."

"Most likely."

"Could it have been an accident? She mistook a plant for something else and that made her sick?"

"Not with the amount she had in her system. It was like someone doused her in the stuff," Campbell said. "This was no accident."

"So, I was right. This was murder."

"Clever you. That doesn't mean I want you poking your nose into this investigation."

"Who have you got on your suspect list? I've spoken to some people who knew Connie. She wasn't popular. In fact, I was just talking to Belinda Adler, and—"

"You don't need to worry about who I have on the suspect list. This case is almost closed."

"What? How come?"

"Because I know what I'm doing."

"So, who killed Connie? Have you charged them?"

"Not yet."

"Are you sure you have the right person? I can help you get a jump on the killer if you're still asking questions. There are only a couple more people I need to speak to before I have information on everyone."

"No! No more speaking to anyone about this. We've got someone we're interested in."

"Is it Tina?"

His mouth twisted, and he looked off into the distance.

"At least give me a clue."

Campbell shook his head, his sharp gaze latching onto mine. "You won't leave this alone until I tell you."

"You know me. I hate loose ends."

"You mean, you always have to know everyone else's business. I need to find you a hobby to keep you out of my way."

"I have plenty of hobbies."

"Hmmm, and I want to talk to you about one of them."

"You do?" I tilted my head. "You want me to teach you how to bake?"

"Funny girl. Not that hobby."

"Stop trying to distract me. You couldn't care less about my hobbies. Who killed Connie?"

"You've already said her name. It was Tina Kennon."

"Oh! The woman causing a scene at the catwalk event. She's got a room at the Walden Inn."

"And how do you know that?"

My stomach clenched, and I looked away. "I must have overheard it somewhere."

"Sure you did." His gaze ran over me. "She's been open about how much she hated Connie. Tina has almost confessed to killing her."

"How did she do it? Did she slip the plant toxin into her coffee?"

"I'm not certain yet." He huffed out a breath. "In fact, I'm not certain she meant to use a plant-based toxin at all. She must have gotten lucky."

"Lucky? Surely you can't just stuff some plants into a person's mouth and watch them die. Didn't you say Connie's system was full of this toxin? That would mean she was given a massive dose just before she died. Were there signs of trauma or injuries that suggest Tina forced the poison into her?"

"No, Miss Marple. But Tina must have figured out a way to give it to Connie. And if it hadn't worked, she had another way to get rid of her."

"What method of murder did Tina have as a backup? She must have been really committed to doing this."

Campbell hummed under his breath.

"I'll only keep asking until you tell me."

"I should have you reassigned."

"Where to?"

"Somewhere far away from me."

"If only you could. It's a shame you aren't my boss." I risked a cheeky grin.

He didn't return it. "If I was, you'd be on insubordination charges."

"Lucky me. So, Tina had plans to murder Connie?"

"She had suspicious items in the trunk of her car when it was searched."

"A backup plan if the poison failed. That's dedication to the cause."

He snorted. "Tina was going to set fire to Connie's display, and most likely Connie. She admitted that she'd come to Audley St. Mary to murder her."

"Connie must have done something terrible to Tina to make her react in such a way."

"You assume right."

I waited for him to expand on the motive, but he remained silent. "Why set fire to the display? That's reckless. Tina could have killed a lot of people, not just Connie."

"Let's just say she's got issues," Campbell said. "She rants and raves about how much she hated Connie and then bursts into tears and says she's sorry. She's having a psychological assessment to ensure she's fit to stand trial." He shifted from foot to foot. "I need to get back to work."

"Hold on, what aren't you telling me? If this case is that simple, you should have charged her already."

"It is simple. Tina's the killer." He looked over my head. "There's just one small problem. Tina has an alibi for the time of Connie's murder."

"Who's her alibi? Maybe they're covering for her. Have you checked their background and made sure they're reliable?"

"I don't need to. It's me."

"Your prime suspect has you as her alibi?" A laugh burst out of me.

"Stop giggling, Holmes."

"Oh, please. I just need to giggle for about ten minutes, then I'll be fine." I wiped my eyes. "What were you doing with Tina?"

He growled at me.

I forced myself to stop laughing. "Okay, I'm being serious. I'd like to know."

"Of course you would." He cracked his knuckles. "I was speaking to Tina about her reckless behavior at the wedding fair when Connie was found. I'm working with the medical examiner to see if we can get an exact time of death. It's possible there was a small window of opportunity for Tina to have killed Connie before we spoke."

"How did she seem when you spoke to her? Surely, if she'd just killed someone, she wouldn't have been calm. You'd have been able to pick up on her nerves."

"That woman is anything but calm, but you're right, she didn't seem like someone who'd just poisoned a person and left the body in a toilet. She was angry rather than upset. And the way she talked about Connie suggested she still thought she was alive. People slip up when they know the truth. Her story has stayed the same. It hasn't changed no matter how many questions I ask her."

"Could she be innocent?"

"No! It's her. I just need to find out how she did it."

"Could Tina have an accomplice? Maybe one of the people I've spoken to."

"She hasn't hinted that anyone else was involved. This is personal. Tina wanted to take Connie down."

"It wouldn't do any harm to speak to some other suspects I've identified, just in case you can't prove it was Tina."

"She's my only suspect," he said. "She did this."

"What's her motive?"

He pressed his lips together.

"You know I'll find out, eventually."

"Connie was sleeping with Tina's husband."

"Oh! That's a great motive." I bit my bottom lip. "When I spoke to Belinda, who knew Connie well, she told me that Connie didn't like to get tied down with one guy."

"Picking married guys to fool around with would guarantee she'd never get tied down," Campbell said. "Tina's been trying to get her to confess for months, but Connie wouldn't admit to anything. That only made her angrier."

"What about the husband?"

"We've been in touch with him. They're separated, but he admitted he was seeing Connie before splitting up with Tina. That's what destroyed the marriage."

"And Tina came to these wedding fairs in the hope of humiliating Connie. Maybe even ruin her business. After all, it doesn't look great if you're in the wedding business but go around ruining other people's marriages."

"She wanted to do much more than ruin the business. Tina had murder on her mind, and she achieved her goal."

"I still think you should speak to some of the others. I wondered if Belinda could be involved. That's why I was talking to her. She was a business rival and had fallen out with Connie after she ditched her. And there's also—"

"Leave me to do my job. Don't you have cakes to ice or something?"

I tutted. "Of course I have. But this is important."

"Yes, I'm aware of that, which is why I'm dealing with it. I have the prime suspect in custody. Tina isn't going anywhere. I just need to figure out how she got such a large dose of poison into Connie."

"I was about to talk to—"

"Enough! No more talk of murder."

I threw up my hands. "Solving this murder should be a priority."

He tipped his head back and rolled his shoulders. "For me! It's my priority. Yours is brownies, bread, and butting out of my business."

"If I bribed you with brownies, would it make a difference?"

"No. Now, forget the murder."

"I can't."

"Try. For five minutes. And until I'm well out of range, so you can't keep questioning me."

"I thought you liked a challenge. Admit it, I keep you on your toes."

"I do. But there's something else I want to talk to you about."

My thoughts went to Granny, and my stomach tightened. "What have I done wrong?"

A rare smile crossed his face. "Nothing, at least not that I know about. I'm interested in your plogging event. I saw the posters up around the village."

"Oh! That! Are you really interested or just trying to distract me from Connie's murder?"

His grin widened. "Maybe a bit of both."

"You want to plog? You know what it is?"

"Of course. I insist my team keep fit. This looks like a good way to get them active. And as you said, I'm always up for some friendly competition."

"You want to compete against me in a plogging event? This is supposed to be for a good cause. Everyone mucks in and helps out. It's not a race to beat each other."

"I know you can never resist trying to get the better of me."

Campbell would beat me hands down in anything that involved physical activity. The man was like a cyborg. He never tired. Still, he was right, I got a great deal of satisfaction out of proving him wrong.

"I'm in. But let's not make it about the distance traveled, though. You don't run far when you plog. How about whoever has the most sacks full of trash is the winner?"

He tilted his head from side to side. "That sounds fair. What does the winner get?"

"You could stop freezing me out of your investigations, admit I'm useful to you, and let me help out."

His face twisted into an expression of disgust. "That's never going to happen. How about, *when* I win, you donate three boxes of cakes to the team?"

"Don't be so sure of yourself. I'm smaller than you and can squeeze into gaps and grab the trash you miss."

"I have nothing to worry about. I always win."

"You don't when it comes to solving murders," I muttered.

He huffed at me. "I should add a caveat to my prize. You stay out of my investigations, but I know I'll be wasting my breath."

"You absolutely will. And don't be so quick to assume Tina's the killer in this case. If she was with you when Connie died, it can't be her. Plus, there are plenty of people at this wedding fair who had a problem with Connie."

He crossed his arms over his chest and shook his head. "Haven't you got somewhere you need to be?"

I did, but I also had murder suspects to question. And if Campbell wasn't going to investigate them, I'd do it for him. And my next target was Connie's spurned lover, Bruce.

Chapter 12

I hurried back into the marquee, to discover Alice still on Belinda's stand, talking excitedly to a wide-eyed couple who couldn't seem to believe who they were speaking to.

When I got closer, I winced. Her conversation wasn't about marriage, but her failed engagements. That was no way to encourage new business.

"You must make sure you pick the right man," Alice said. "I still haven't gotten the hang of it. I'll get there, eventually. You make an adorable couple."

"I expect there are dozens of men asking for your hand in marriage," the brunette in front of her said.

"All the time, but they're all boring, old, or lazy. I don't care how rich they are or how much land they own, I must love them. How did you know your fiancé was the right one?" she asked.

"Well, we've been together for ages. It seemed like the right thing to do when he asked me to marry him," the woman stammered.

"Plus, we love each other," the man by her side said. "You'll find someone who is right for you. You're stunning."

His fiancée shot him a glare. "Let's go. This isn't the right stand for us." She dragged him away.

"Having fun?" I asked Alice as I joined her at the stand.

"Not really. I don't think I've got the hang of this wedding promotion. And everyone keeps staring at me as if I've grown a second head. I decided to try a different tactic and talk about my own experience with relationships. Although that's not going too well, either."

"No kidding." I grinned at her. "If you're done here, I've got some information you might want to hear."

"Of course. Belinda came back a little while ago. She's out the back getting some more leaflets. She seemed pretty down. Did you get anything useful out of her?"

"Only that I don't think she killed Connie. They had their problems, but she was really shocked when she learned it was murder."

"Possibly murder." Alice walked along beside me through the growing crowd.

"No, that's my big bit of news. Campbell caught me talking to Belinda. He reluctantly told me that Connie was poisoned by a plant toxin."

Alice clapped a hand over her mouth. When she lowered it, she was smiling. "How exciting. I love a good murder."

"You worry me, sometimes."

"Oh, you know what I mean. I love the mystery and finding the clues. It's fun watching you snoop about and figure it all out."

"Well, thanks, I guess. I like to make sure a wrong is put right."

"Of course. So, what's our next move?"

"First off, we need to check Belinda's alibi." I glanced around to make sure Belinda was out of sight. I hurried over to her laptop, which was tucked under the counter. "She said she was ordering flowers at the time of the murder." I opened her search history and found the time

Connie's body was found. There was a record of her on a flower wholesaler site at the time. So far, her alibi stuck.

"What are you looking for?" Alice peered over my shoulder.

"Is Belinda's phone around?"

Alice scooped it out from under the desk. "Here it is. Why do you need it?"

I was relieved that it wasn't password protected. I scrolled through her call list. "She said she was on the phone when Connie was found. Look! She was telling the truth. This call lasted just over ten minutes, and the number matches the flower wholesaler on their website."

"What about the other woman, Tina?" Alice said as she placed the phone and laptop away for me.

"Campbell has her in custody. She's raging mad with Connie because she was sleeping with her husband."

Alice sighed. "Which means the case is closed. The killer's been caught."

"Nope, Campbell's her alibi. Tina can't have done it, even though he's refusing to accept that. We need to speak to the other suspects. When I was talking to Belinda, she mentioned Connie used to date one of the wine merchants. We met him when we were looking around with Diana. Apparently, he has a bit of a temper and an unhealthy obsession with Connie."

"That sounds like the killer we're looking for. Let's go and quiz him," Alice said. "Oh, and before I forget, there was a lady asking about you. She seemed to know you. She was older, quite sophisticated looking. She had big sunglasses on, even though we're inside and it's not that sunny today."

It sounded like Granny Molly hadn't stuck to her end of the deal and had left my apartment. I couldn't blame her, she probably didn't like being cooped up in small places.

But I needed to keep an eye on her if she was out and about.

"I don't know who that could be. Come on, let's speak to Bruce. I have to get back to the kitchen soon, or I'll get in trouble with Chef Heston."

We headed into the food marquee and over to Bruce's display.

He smiled broadly when he saw us. "Princess Alice, it's so generous of you to come and see me again. May I tempt you with some samples of something rich and full-bodied?"

"It's a little early for me," Alice said.

"Of course. Such a charming lady must know her limits. At least allow me to give you a bottle of my finest Merlot. Compliments of Osman Vineyard. Perhaps you could have it at dinner tonight and think of me while you take a sip."

"That sounds delicious. You know just how to tempt someone. Are you always this flirty with your customers?" Alice asked.

"Only the ones I have an affinity with." His smile broadened. "And, if I may be so bold, I'd be delighted to visit your family and present them with a complimentary selection of my wines."

Alice's eyes sparkled. "That's a fun idea. We could have a wine tasting evening."

I nudged her. "Maybe we can discuss the wine later."

"Oh! Yes." Alice nodded. "Actually, we have a few questions about Connie. I believe you knew her."

Bruce sighed. "I did. Such a loss. I can't believe she's gone."

"You were close?" I asked.

"Very. What do you want to know about her?" he said.

"Did you know, she was murdered?" Alice said in a loud whisper.

Bruce stared at her, his mouth open. "I ... I don't understand."

"There's been some evidence uncovered during the autopsy," I said. "Connie's death wasn't an accident."

The color drained from Bruce's face. He swayed from side to side.

I raced behind the display and caught hold of him before he crashed into the bottles of wine. "Are you okay?"

"No, I'm very much not okay." He gasped in a breath. "Are you sure about this? Where did you hear this terrible news?"

"Let's sit down for a moment. Alice, keep an eye on the wine."

She grinned and nodded, before turning to the stand. "Princess Alice's fine wines and drunken escapades is open for business. Come get your free samples."

I led a shaking Bruce to a chair at the back of the display and settled him on it. "Put your head between your knees if you're feeling faint."

He did as instructed, gasping in a big breath of air. "What happened to Connie?" He raised his head and stared at me, his eyes wide.

"Connie was definitely killed. The police are investigating the details."

He shook his head. "How do you know this? You knew Connie?"

"No, but I work ... closely with the security in the castle." Bruce didn't need to know it was in an unwelcome and unofficial capacity.

"Oh, are you Princess Alice's bodyguard? It's not unusual to employ someone small and unassuming to look after a princess. I've witnessed it when I've supplied wine and champagne for socialites' weddings. It helps you blend in if you're unremarkable looking."

"Unremarkable looking? Well, I suppose so. Yes, that's … that's what I do." I wasn't going to pull him up on his rude comment while he was talking, but I hated being called unremarkable. "It's important we make sure the wedding fair is safe for everyone, especially the family. What was your relationship with Connie?"

His gaze narrowed. "You've been talking to the other stallholders. They've told you about us."

"I'm more interested in learning what you have to tell me. You and Connie used to be in a relationship?"

"As far as I was concerned, we never broke up. I loved the woman. We were a golden couple, the kind other people aspire to be like. We could have been so happy together if she'd just given up her party lifestyle. Connie couldn't see how good we were. But it was only a matter of time before she figured out that she'd never find somebody better than me."

Or someone as modest and tactful. "Where did you see the relationship going?"

"I planned to marry her. I proposed several times, but Connie could be so coy. She turned down my proposals, but it was only because she wanted to make me keener. And it worked. I couldn't stop thinking about ways to win her over."

"You thought Connie's rejection was a sign she was interested in you?"

Bruce's nostrils flared. "It wasn't rejection. She was a passionate woman and full of confidence. She liked to pretend she didn't need a man in her life, but I could see that wasn't true. I made her happy. We enjoyed our time together."

"You don't think she simply didn't want to get married?"

He spread his hands out, his confident smile returning. "I'm a catch. I have plenty of women interested in me, but

I'd set my sights on Connie. I was determined she'd be mine."

"Bruce, sorry to interrupt." A tall guy with glasses appeared from around the side of the display. "I hope I'm not interrupting. I heard your voice. I need the details about that case of Chardonnay you promised me. I've got a couple waiting for it."

"Not now," Bruce said. "I'm in the middle of something."

"You were supposed to bring it over half an hour ago. I really—"

"I told you, I'm busy. Get lost." Bruce's hands clenched into fists.

The guy glared at him before walking away. "It's your loss, idiot."

Bruce shook his head and his fingers relaxed. "Sorry about that. I'm still in shock over what you told me about Connie. Murder. Really?"

"I imagine you are, especially if you had plans to marry."

He rolled his shoulders and cracked his neck. "Who did this? Give me a name and I'll make them pay."

"There's an ongoing investigation. The police have someone they're interested in, but I'm covering all the bases to make sure nothing is missed."

"The thought of someone hurting my woman, I'll tear their head off." He wiped a hand across his forehead. "Connie was a great girl. One-of-a-kind."

"Can you tell me where you were when Connie's body was discovered?"

He tapped a finger against his chin. "You're checking the boyfriend wasn't involved? It makes sense. I've seen plenty of crime dramas on TV. They always look to the partner first. I'm afraid you're wasting your time if you want me on the suspect list. I was with Zoe Rossini when I heard the news."

I'd heard that name before from Leanna. "She has a business at the wedding fair?"

"That's right. She used to work with Connie. She's in wedding planning these days, not flowers. A charming woman. Very easy on the eye, although not much in the brains department."

Wow, he was a charmless guy. No wonder Connie ditched him. "What were you doing with Zoe? You're just friends?"

His smile turned smarmy. "A man needs to keep his options open. Connie was proving to be a challenge, so I needed a backup plan."

"Does Zoe know she was your backup plan?"

"Most things pass over Zoe's head. It's nothing I need to trouble her with. But I'll have to re-think things now. With Connie gone, I have a hole in my life that needs to be filled."

So much for everlasting love. Bruce had gone from shocked to angry to searching for a new girlfriend in the space of five minutes. This guy was a piece of work.

"Thanks for your time," I said. "I'll leave you to it. I expect you have a busy day ahead of you." No doubt it would involve creeping on female customers and leering at women.

"Keep me up-to-date about what's going on. Connie was practically my wife. I must be the first to know who killed her."

"You'll definitely be hearing from me." Especially if he was involved with what happened to Connie.

I left him on the seat to 'recover' and returned to Alice, who was pouring out rather large glasses of wine for people to try.

"We need to leave," I whispered to her.

She placed the wine bottle down. "Did Bruce tell you anything useful?"

I glanced over my shoulder. "Yes, but I can't tell you here in case he overhears us."

"That sounds exciting. I've seen some frosted carrot cake I'd love to try," Alice said. "We deserve a treat after all this investigating."

"What have you been investigating? How quickly you can get people drunk?"

She giggled as she handed over a glass of wine to a waiting customer. "Everyone is having a great time. I've emptied ten bottles."

I grinned. That wouldn't make Bruce happy. It was no less than he deserved.

We got two large slices of carrot cake and two cups of tea and settled on a table out of earshot of anyone else.

Alice forked a piece of cake into her mouth. "It's good. Not as good as yours, of course. So, what did Bruce tell you? I thought he was going to pass out when he heard about Connie's murder."

"It maybe wasn't the best idea to blurt that out to him."

"It was. It got his attention."

"True. And he was willing to talk, especially because he thinks I'm your bodyguard."

Alice spluttered a laugh. "Hilarious. Campbell will throw a fit when he learns you're pretending to be on his team."

"I didn't say that as such, but Bruce assumed and I played along. It meant he didn't think it odd that I was asking questions about Connie."

"So, what's the news?"

"Bruce planned to get Connie to marry him, but she had other ideas. She turned him down several times."

"Some men can't take a hint," Alice said. "I've got one suitor at the moment, an aging Belgian prince, who must have asked for my hand in marriage a dozen times. I've tried saying no politely, being rude to his face, sending him a very stern letter, and returned all his gifts, yet he still persists. I don't know whether he's stubborn or stupid."

"I get the impression Bruce is stubborn. He sets his eyes on a prize and won't give up until he gets it. Which could have meant bad news for Connie. She wasn't interested in him, so he decided if he couldn't have her, no one else would."

"That's repulsive. And he seemed like such a charming man."

"I'm not buying into the charm. It's just an act. He has to go on the suspect list. Bruce was at the wedding fair at the same time as Connie. She knew him and trusted him. It would have been easy to get close to her and give her the poison."

"It's such a cowardly way to kill someone," Alice said. "Sneaky, too. If I ever murder someone, I want to look them in the eye and tell them why they're about to die."

I snorted a shocked laugh. "Do you have any plans like that?"

Alice chuckled. "Don't worry. I'll never kill you, so long as you keep making me your delicious cakes."

"That's a relief." I ate some carrot cake. Alice and her dark thoughts were often a concern. How could someone so sweet also be so terrifying? "Bruce strikes me as a sneaky kind of guy. Not only is he sneaky, he's also controlling and has a temper. He yelled at some guy who came in asking for his wine order when we were talking. I can easily imagine when Connie rejected him that he refused to accept it."

"Which puts him at the top of the list of suspects," Alice said.

"There's a small problem we need to clear up before we do that. Bruce claims to have an alibi. He was with a wedding planner when Connie's body was found."

"That'll be easy to check," Alice said. "Let's find this woman after we've had our cake and ask if he was telling the truth."

My fork froze halfway to my mouth. Granny Molly had appeared in the crowd. She was wearing her dark glasses again and a scarf over her head, but I spotted her straightaway.

"We'll have to put the investigation on hold for a little while." I dropped my fork.

"Why? And you've barely touched your cake. Is something wrong with it?"

I pushed my plate over to her and stood. "You have it. I need to be somewhere. I'll catch up with you later."

"Oh! Very well." Alice's forehead wrinkled. "Is everything okay?"

"Yes. I'm just not in the mood for cake."

"I suppose they are only small pieces." She scooped up my cake. "I can manage both."

"Great. I'll see you later." I hurried away, scanning the crowd for Granny Molly. I needed to keep an eye on her. If she was on the loose, trouble wouldn't be far behind. And I couldn't risk her causing problems for me. Not when I needed to focus on this murder.

Chapter 13

Despite searching through the crowd for ten minutes, I lost sight of Granny Molly.

Worry rumbled through me. She'd better not be lifting more purses from well-heeled visitors. I had to find her and get her back to my apartment. Maybe I could leave Meatball with her. He'd keep her entertained and make her less likely to stray toward trouble.

I was about to give up my search, when I spotted her. My stomach flipped over and I groaned. She was talking to Betsy Malone. This was bad news. Betsy would fill her in on all the village gossip. And maybe Granny Molly would share some of her secrets, too.

I couldn't help but feel a little guilty that I was ashamed of her past. I hadn't told anyone about her. I didn't want people knowing she was a criminal. I loved her, but she'd broken the law. She'd served her time but had already proven she wasn't a reformed character.

If word got back to the Duke and Duchess, and they decided they didn't want the granddaughter of a criminal working for them, I could lose everything. Sometimes, families were so tricky to handle.

K.E. O'CONNOR

My phone buzzed, and I pulled it out, before opening the message from Chef Heston.

You're five minutes late. Get your behind into the kitchen right now if you want to keep your job.

I checked the time and gasped. I'd been so busy hunting clues for Connie's murder that I've lost track of how late it had gotten.

I briefly considered chasing after Granny Molly, but I was out of time. I had to abandon my gran and this investigation if I wanted to stay employed.

I dashed out of the crowd and raced to the kitchen, hoping Chef Heston wouldn't yell too loudly when I arrived.

Murder would have to wait. Muffins were now my priority.

※※※※※ ※※※※※

I swiped a hand across my forehead and rolled my shoulders. Chef Heston had worked me extra hard this afternoon because I'd been late back from lunch.

I'd kneaded bread until my arm muscles had burned, but I was proud of the dozen fresh loaves that sat cooling in front of me.

"We should go take a look," one of the kitchen assistants said to her friend as they hurried past. "Apparently, they've taken over the pub and are singing songs."

I lifted my head. Who were they talking about?

"She must be a friend of Betsy's who's come for a visit."

"No one knows who she is. But she bought a round of drinks for everyone in the pub, so she must be fun. Come on, let's go over there and see if she's still around. We might get a free drink, too."

My stomach lurched. The strange woman with Betsy must be Gran. What was she doing spending her money on buying drinks for everyone? That was no way to keep a low profile. She'd get us both in trouble if she wasn't careful.

I checked over my to-do list, happy to see all my tasks were done, tidied away my equipment, and removed my apron, before heading out into the cool evening air.

"Come on Meatball, we're on a mission to save Gran from embarrassing herself, and me."

I grabbed the delivery bike from the storage shed, placed Meatball in his basket, secured the helmet on his head, and then pushed off.

I raced along the lanes of Audley St. Mary, pumping my legs as I hit the hills, my stomach a riot of nerves. Granny Molly had always been terrible with money. She was generous with everyone and used to be way too trusting for her own good. That was how she'd gotten in so much trouble. A smooth-talking jerk had convinced her he loved her. The problem was, he'd only loved her money. He'd taken everything and left her with a ton of debt, before sneaking off to live a life of luxury on her dime.

So, Gran got inventive and decided to focus her money making efforts on the opposite sex. She figured it was a way to heal her broken heart. She targeted wealthy older men, often just stealing their wallets, but sometimes she took more. She'd been successful for a while. She cleared her debts and got herself back on her feet. Then she got caught.

I stopped the bike outside the pub and climbed off. I unclipped Meatball's harness, took off his helmet, and tucked him under my arm, before heading inside.

A wave of noise and raucous singing hit me as I pulled the door open.

There was a small crowd gathered in the center of the pub.

As I eased my way through, I discovered they were looking at Betsy and my gran as they drunkenly performed *You Can Leave Your Hat On* by Tom Jones.

I grimaced. There was a lot of unsavory gyrating going on.

Granny Molly twirled in a circle. She staggered to one side, her gaze met mine, and a huge smile crossed her face. "Holly! I hope you're here to join in the fun with everyone else."

I pushed past a couple of people and caught hold of her arm. "I thought I told you to stay in the apartment."

She hugged me and kissed my cheek. "I got bored. I decided to take a look around the wedding fair."

I pulled back from her hug. "You're sure that was all you were doing?"

She wrinkled her brow and frowned at me. "I promised you I'd behave myself."

"Molly, get back over here," Betsy shouted. "We've got another verse to sing."

Gran waved a hand at Betsy. "You finish. Let me get you a drink, Holly."

"Let's go back to mine. I'll make some dinner and you can sober up."

"I don't want to go home," Granny Molly said. "The people in this village are so friendly. I can see why you moved here."

I glanced around the crowd in the pub. "Have you been spending your money buying them drinks?"

"You know me, I take from the rich and give to the poor."

"Shush! Be careful what you say."

She hugged me again. "You're such a good girl. Always looking out for me."

Betsy finished her out of tune singing and stumbled over, her cheeks bright pink and a glass in one hand. "You never told me you had such a fun gran, Holly. Why haven't you invited her to stay before?"

"Um, well, she's been away," I said.

"Traveling. I like to spend the winters somewhere warm. But you're right, my visit to see Holly was long overdue. I'm glad I came." Gran winked at me.

"If you're looking for a place to settle down, Audley St. Mary is it. I'll never leave here," Betsy said. "And if you're ever looking for a job, I need reliable people on my cleaning team at the castle. I'd be happy to take you on. We'd have such fun together."

"A job at the castle." Gran's eyes widened. "Fancy that. Holly, we could work together."

I wasn't sure how I felt about that. If Granny Molly got a job, it could keep her on the straight and narrow, but what if being inside the castle, surrounded by all the valuable antiques, was too much of a temptation?

"Let's talk about that tomorrow when you both have clear heads," I said.

"Have you made any progress with that poor girl's murder?" Granny Molly said far too loudly, causing several people to look over.

"Oh, yes! Tell us all about it." Betsy huddled closer. "It's all people are gossiping about. I couldn't believe it when I heard she'd been poisoned."

"Where did you hear that?" I asked.

"One of my girls back at the castle overheard the security team talking."

"What did they say?" Despite not enjoying gossiping, it had its uses.

"Apparently, it was a plant called ragwort that was used to kill her. My girl heard them say she had a lot of plant toxin in her system."

"Didn't she work with flowers?" Granny Molly asked. "She should know what could poison her, and avoid it."

"She'd be a terrible flower arranger if she didn't know what would make her clients sick." Betsy chortled and sipped from her glass. "I've got an idea. Maybe it was injected into her. I saw that in a movie. They hid the injection site between—" She burst out laughing. "The poor man. They injected him between his bum cheeks to hide the hole!"

"That's terrible!" Granny Molly joined in the laughter.

"Not so funny for Connie if that's what happened to her." I tried to sound stern but failed. Their laughter was infectious.

Betsy wiped her eyes. "No, you're right. It was a horrible thing to happen."

"I wonder if any injection sites were found on the body during the autopsy," I said. "They may not have been looking for marks like that when they examined Connie."

"Your granddaughter certainly has a morbid fascination with the dead," Betsy said. "It's served her well in the past, though. If it wasn't for young Holly, there'd be several unsolved murders at the castle."

I glanced around. "Don't let Campbell or the police hear that. They won't be happy if people think they don't know how to do their jobs."

"Pah! They don't. You're always telling Campbell what to do," Betsy said.

"I'd never dare do that. I simply make gentle suggestions if I think he's going in the wrong direction when a crime's been committed." I touched Granny Molly's arm. "Let's go home. There are things we need to talk about." I lifted my eyebrows and gestured to the door.

"It sounds like you're in trouble." Betsy laughed heartily. "Still, I need to get back, too. I thought we'd only be here for half an hour. I didn't realize how late it had gotten."

After much hugging and a lot of farewells, I managed to get Granny Molly and Betsy out of the pub.

I placed Meatball back in the basket on the front of the bike and wheeled it beside them as they staggered along, holding each other up and occasionally breaking into song.

"I was thinking about this poisoning business," Betsy said. "If you want to know more about the plant that killed that woman, you should speak to Ray. Our head gardener knows everything about plants. He's always quick to tell me not to pick things because it'll disturb the growing cycle. I let him off because he's a handsome devil and has a mischievous twinkle in his eye. If you're looking for information about ragwort, he's the man to go to."

I nodded. I didn't know much about poisonous plants. An expert on side would be helpful. "Thanks, Betsy. I'll speak to him tomorrow."

We helped Betsy back to her tiny cottage, then said goodbye.

"Are you okay to walk back to the castle?" I asked Gran. "We could get a cab."

"Of course. I don't mind walking. Unless you want to sit me on your handlebars and cycle us home." She laughed and wrapped an arm around my shoulders.

"Walking it is." I grinned at her.

"You're not angry with me, are you?" she said after a moment.

"Why would you think that?"

"Well, I said I'd stay in your apartment. The thing is, now I have my freedom, I want to explore. I made a big show of not minding going to prison, how I got free meals and a safe place to sleep, but …"

I nodded. "You always said it was like a strict holiday camp."

"It was, most of the time. Minimal security places aren't that stressful, but there's nothing like having your freedom and making your own decisions. I got a bit carried away today. I didn't mean to embarrass you."

"You didn't! And I do get it. I'm not angry with you, I'm just worried about you getting in trouble and losing your newfound freedom."

"More like you're worried about what people think of me." Granny Molly shrugged and lowered her head. "Betsy didn't even know I was your granny. You've never told anyone about me?"

I looked away. "I wasn't sure what to tell them."

"That your old gran made a foolish mistake."

"Does that mean you're turning over a new leaf? No more stealing?"

She laughed. "No, the mistake was I got caught. I learned a lot more than bookkeeping while I was inside. I definitely won't make that mistake again."

I sighed. No matter what I said, Granny Molly would never change. She was a rogue, but a loveable one.

"Now, I want to hear more about your skills in detecting murderers," Gran said.

"They're not skills, as such. I just notice things about people. And I like asking questions and finding out what makes them tick."

"Go on, start at the beginning. We've got quite a walk ahead of us."

I smiled. We did, given how slowly Gran was walking.

As I talked about my amateur skills, I rolled around the plant poison idea some more. I needed to speak to Ray and learn all about ragwort. First thing in the morning, I'd get right on that. Maybe then I'd figure out who poisoned Connie, how they did it, and why.

Chapter 14

I was up early the next day and out in the fresh morning air, walking Meatball as the sun was climbing over the treetops.

I'd left Gran sleeping off her previous evening's indulgences. She'd most likely have a sore head when she surfaced.

"This way, Meatball." I turned from our usual path that led into the trees. I wanted to find Ray and chat to him about all things ragwort related.

We headed past the ornamental rose garden and into the private family gardens. This area of the grounds was technically off-limits to anyone other than the family, but the Duchess didn't mind staff walking around and enjoying the beautiful space. There was an organic fruit orchard, a vast wildflower meadow, and a huge space dedicated to lavender. It was stunning when all the blooms were out, and the air buzzed with nectar-collecting insects.

Meatball trotted along beside me, exploring the garden as we made our way along the stone path.

"Morning," I said as I spotted one of the gardeners pushing a wheelbarrow.

He turned and lifted a hand.

"Is Ray here yet?" I asked.

"Over by the potting shed," the guy said.

I nodded a thanks and headed past the greenhouses and over to three large green sheds.

Meatball barked, his ears pricking up. He raced through one of the open doors.

"Come back. You're not supposed to be in there." I hurried over to the shed and pulled open the door wider.

I discovered Meatball sitting obediently in front of a tall guy wearing gardening overalls and a flat cap. I recognized him straight away. It was Ray Smith.

He looked up as I entered, a dog biscuit in one hand. "Morning, Holly. Is this little fellow not following your instructions?"

"It wouldn't be the first time. When he gets that determined glint in his eyes, I don't stand a chance." I walked into the potting shed, the smell of compost hitting me. "It looks like you two are friends."

Ray grinned. He was in his early fifties and had a face that looked like he'd spent most of his life outdoors. "You could say that. Meatball comes over here some days and spends time with me."

"He does?" I looked down at Meatball. He wagged his tail at me. "I never knew that."

"I've seen him in his kennel outside the kitchen," Ray said. "We got talking one day, and he decided to follow me into the garden."

"You are full of surprises," I said to Meatball. "When I'm busy in the kitchen, I figured he simply went to sleep."

"I expect he does most of the time, and he doesn't come out here much in the winter, but he likes to have a root around while I'm dealing with the plants. He chased out some rats once."

"And I see he's got you feeding him," I said.

Ray gave Meatball the dog biscuit. "He's got me well-trained. I used to have my own dog. She was a wonderful old thing. Loved long walks and sitting by the fire with me in the pub."

"She's not around, anymore?"

He petted Meatball. "She got sick. I had to have her put to sleep."

My hand went to my chest, and I pressed it against my heart. "I'm so sorry."

He ducked his head. "Darn near broke me when I had to let her go. I miss not having her around. I enjoy Meatball's company. It reminds me of how good it is to have a dog."

"He seems happy to be here," I said.

"I like to think he is." Ray pushed his cap back. "I don't see you in this part of the garden very often. Is there something you need?"

"There is. I've got a few questions about a plant. I wonder if you can help me."

"Don't see why not? You're getting into gardening?"

"Nothing like that. I have my hands full in the kitchen. Although I often use the fresh produce in my baking."

"And I enjoy sampling the cakes you make with that produce," Ray said. "You baked some lavender scones not so long ago. I keep checking to see if they're back in the café."

I grinned. "I'll put them on the list of customer requests."

He rubbed his hands together. "I'll be first in line. So, what plant are you interested in?"

"Ragwort. What can you tell me about it?"

His eyebrows shot up. "That you definitely don't want to use it in your cooking. It's poisonous."

"Does it grow around here?" I asked.

"Sure. It's easy to cultivate. We have a lot of it in the grounds because it's great for the bees and the pollinators.

It's not so human friendly."

"Is it easy to grow?"

His expression was full of curiosity. "Yep. It does best when left on its own. It hates being cultivated. Ragwort is basically a pretty weed. It has small yellow flowers in the summer. It's nice enough to look at. Most people simply yank it up and throw it away. You won't find me doing that here, but I make sure it's not in any of the public areas, just in case. It's not such a problem if you only come into contact with it now and again, but you don't want to handle ragwort every day."

"Is it only poisonous if you eat it?"

"No. You need to wear gloves when you're dealing with it. It can be absorbed through the skin, but not in a way to make you really ill. Better to be safe, though."

"Does the plant need to be fresh for it to be toxic?"

He scrubbed at his chin. "No. You could dry ragwort and use it in a powdered form. I can't imagine why anyone would want to do that. It's a bitter tasting plant. In a concentrated form like that, it would be disgusting."

"Say someone came into regular contact with ragwort and didn't realize it. Could it build up in their system and make them unwell?"

He rubbed the back of his neck. "Absolutely. What are you thinking? Someone you know handled ragwort and got ill from it?"

"Maybe not handled it." I considered all the herbs I used from the garden in my baking. "Could they have eaten it in small doses over time? Would that make a person ill?"

"Yes, but that would be hard to do. That stuff is foul. Even if you hid it in something sweet, you'd most likely taste the bitterness. What's with all the questions about ragwort?"

"I don't know if you've heard, but someone died at the wedding fair."

"I did. It's all my team keep talking about. She was a wedding planner, wasn't she?"

"Connie dealt with wedding flowers," I said. "Could she have mistaken ragwort for something else? Maybe she was using it in her bouquets and didn't realize what it was."

Ray shook his head. "I can't see that happening. Anyone who knows their flowers will know to be careful around ragwort. Besides, it's not what you'd call a pretty plant. You wouldn't put it in a bride's bouquet. She couldn't have made a mistake like that. Did this woman die because she came into contact with ragwort?"

I nodded. "It's possible. She had a high level of plant toxins in her system. I figured she'd come into contact with a massive dose and it killed her. But if it could build up over time, maybe she'd been around it for a while."

He puffed out a breath. "If that's the case, she can't have been an experienced florist."

"Connie had been in the business for years."

"If that's the case, her getting poisoned by ragwort doesn't sound accidental."

"That's what I'm wondering. What are the symptoms of ragwort poisoning?"

"I don't know offhand, but give me a minute, I'll take a look in my books." Ray gave Meatball another biscuit. He walked to the back of the shed and pulled out a large encyclopedia of plants. He placed it on a clean, well-worn oak potting table and flipped it open. "This is my bible. If ever I have questions about plants, this is where I come."

I walked over and inspected the thumbed pages of the book.

He flipped through the pages and ran a finger along the text. "Here we are, ragwort. The symptoms include an upset stomach, feeling sick, headache, occasionally a yellow tinge to the skin. If untreated, a person can die, but that's really rare."

"I saw Connie stumbling around. I assumed she'd been drinking. Is poor balance a side-effect of ragwort poisoning?"

"Yep. That's listed in here," Ray said. "And if she was already suffering symptoms because she had so much in her system, it would have been difficult to save her. Ragwort can damage vital organs if left untreated."

"That's good to know. Thanks, Ray. I appreciate the information."

"You're welcome. Why the interest? Did you know the woman who died?"

"Not well."

He lifted his chin and his warm gaze traveled over me, a smile on his face as he turned to Meatball. "Is your mom looking into another mystery?"

"Woof, woof!" Meatball wagged his tail.

"What makes you say that?" I asked.

"I've heard a thing or two about you. You like poking around in mysteries," Ray said.

My cheeks grew warm. "Have you been talking to Campbell?"

He chuckled. "I may have heard something about you from Campbell."

"I doubt anything he said about me was good."

"It wasn't all bad. Don't mind his sternness. He's laser focused on protecting the family. That's his mission. The man is a machine. If he thinks you're getting in the way of achieving his goal, you'll be in trouble."

"He shouldn't be so quick to dismiss me. I have helped him in the past. And Campbell isn't perfect."

"None of us are. I expect you set him straight when he goes wrong."

"Only when he's being really stubborn."

Ray grinned. "Good for you. Now, I'd better get on, unless you have more questions about ragwort. I've got two hundred plants to get dug in today."

"No. That information could be really helpful." I thanked him again, smiling indulgently as Meatball begged for one more biscuit, before we left.

"Holly! What are you doing in this part of the garden?" Rupert ambled over, a smile on his face.

I fell into step with him as we walked past the roses. "I was talking to Ray about ragwort. It's the plant that poisoned Connie."

"I heard from Alice that she was killed. It sounds like a nasty way to die," Rupert said.

"I agree. And I think she was struggling with the side effects of being slowly poisoned for a while. When we met, I thought she just had a stomach bug, but whoever was giving her ragwort wanted to ensure she suffered. I think they slowly built up the toxin to make her sick without her getting worried. The symptoms must have come on gradually until the killer decided to strike and give her a final fatal dose."

Rupert grimaced. "Whoever it was, they sound calculating."

I nodded. "And they must have been in Connie's life on a regular basis. They'd have needed to drip feed her poison over several months to sicken her slowly."

He touched my arm. "Holly, perhaps you should leave this mystery alone. This person is dangerous."

"I have to know who killed Connie. Campbell has someone in custody, but I'm not convinced it's her, and he's not looking at any other suspects."

Rupert hummed under his breath. "I figured you'd say as much. Well, if you need help to find out who did it, I'm around. I could be your Watson, Holmes."

I laughed. "Nice idea. Especially since I'm not sure which way to turn right now."

"Then I'm your man. And I need something to keep me occupied. I'm avoiding my parents. And other than my brief appearance on the catwalk with you, I've been keeping a low profile at the wedding fair so they don't keep getting ideas about marrying me off. Let me help you solve this mystery. It'll give me something positive to focus on."

"Surely your future wedding is something to look forward to, not hide from."

He hummed again. "It depends who I'm marrying. Besides, it would be nice to spend more time together. Alice always monopolizes you."

I was about to accept his offer, when I spotted Campbell up ahead, lurking by a bush. Even though there was no way he could have overheard us, he was shooting me daggers. If I got Rupert involved in this mystery, Campbell would be on my back, chastising me for putting the family at risk.

"It's probably not a good idea that you help," I said.

"Oh! But Alice is always helping you. I figured a fresh pair of eyes looking at the evidence could be what you need."

"Maybe another time, Rupert." I stopped walking and turned to him. "And maybe you should go to the wedding fair. You might find inspiration strikes."

His expression turned quizzical. "Inspiration? You're also suggesting I should get married? Why does everyone want to see me settled so badly?"

"It's what your parents want. And it's not such a bad idea. You don't want to be on your own."

He shook his head. "I'm not on my own. I have my family around me, and my friends, and I have you."

And that was the problem. I liked Rupert, we were friends, but it wasn't hard to see that there was something more than friendship between us. It was just too much of a risk. What if we went on a date and it went wrong? It would be so awkward working at the castle and seeing Rupert every day. And then there was the not insignificant issue of our different social status. This may be a modern world, but kitchen assistants simply didn't get involved with future owners of enormous castles, no matter how sweet that future castle owner was.

"Have I said something wrong?" Rupert asked. "I thought you'd appreciate my help."

"I do, but you'd better not get involved in this mystery. It could all be over soon, anyway, and I'm worrying about nothing."

He tugged at his bottom lip. "Not according to Alice. She said it can't possibly be the woman the police are holding. If you don't want me to help, you just need to say. I don't want to get in your way."

"No! It's not that. It's just that …" I couldn't tell him I didn't want to develop stronger feelings for him. And I would if we kept spending time together. There wasn't a bad thing about Rupert.

He sighed. "You think I'd get in the way. Don't worry, I can take a hint. I'll see you around." Rupert strode away, his shoulders down and his hands in his pockets.

"Oh dear," I said to Meatball. "I could have handled that better. You understand, don't you?"

"Woof." That sounded like a definite no.

I pushed thoughts of Rupert to one side as I marched along with Meatball back to my apartment. It felt so much easier to poke about in a murder than try to figure out my route to happiness with a lord.

"I'll focus on the thing I can do something about," I muttered.

"Woof, woof?" Meatball tilted his head from side to side.

"If this poison was administered over a long time, potentially, the suspects I've spoken to could be involved. If they had regular access to Connie, they could have given her the poison in small doses."

Meatball wagged his tail in agreement. Well, it could have been agreement, or he could have been thinking about the tasty snacks Ray had fed him.

"Which means it's even less likely that Tina killed Connie. She wouldn't have seen her regularly. Although it does sound like she hounded her for months to get her to admit she was sleeping with her husband. But would she have had an opportunity to slip poison into Connie's food or drink while she was doing that? It doesn't seem likely, does it?"

"Woof!"

"Belinda would have seen Connie all the time if they were doing the same wedding circuit. And then there's Bruce. He was obsessed with Connie and followed her to the same wedding fairs. There's also Leanna." I shook my head. "These suspects need looking at again. One of them had a serious problem with Connie, which led to them inflicting a horrible death on her."

"Woof, woof."

"So, rather than complicated marriages, let's concentrate on a complex murder."

Chapter 15

"Hurry up with those cakes." Chef Heston marched past my workstation in the kitchen, a scowl on his face and his shoulders tight.

We'd been rushed off our feet all day. The orders hadn't stopped coming in, and I still needed to finish decorating my medieval wedding cake. It was going out on the Audley Castle display this afternoon as part of the celebrations. The cake still needed icing and the decorations finishing off. I wasn't sure I'd be able to fit everything in, and there was a queue to get in the café for afternoon tea.

I inspected my next tasks on my to-do list. Cherry scones, bilberry tarts, and blueberry blast muffins.

"Get a move on, Holly," Chef Heston said. "I need four dozen cherry scones, and those ginger tarts need icing."

"On it, Chef." I raced over to the table and assembled my icing bag.

Campbell strode into the kitchen. Granny Molly was beside him.

My heart sped up as I saw he had hold of her arm and wasn't looking happy, although that was his default expression. "I don't have time to give you free food today."

"I'm not here for a free muffin. This woman claims to know you." Campbell pointed at Granny Molly.

I glanced at her. I had no idea what she'd told him about our connection. "That's right. Is there a problem?"

"She's been selling raffle tickets at the wedding fair."

"Of course I have," Granny Molly said. "We have a grand prize for the winner."

"We've never done that before," Campbell said. "I wasn't informed there'd be a raffle."

"Why would anyone tell you?" I asked. "Raffles don't fall under security tasks."

He grunted. "It's still not on the agenda. And there's no mention of a raffle on the promotional materials."

I waved my icing bag in the air. "It's fine. There's nothing to worry about."

"You'll vouch for this woman?" Campbell asked.

I sucked in a deep breath. "Of course. She's not doing anything wrong. You probably terrified her by dragging her out of the wedding fair."

His eyes narrowed as if he could tell I wasn't being totally honest. "You can't be too careful."

"I agree. Since you're here, have you got time to talk about Connie?" I asked.

Campbell let go of Granny Molly's arm. "No. I've got work to do." He turned and strode away.

Granny Molly shook her head and chuckled. "He's certainly lacking in the humor department. No matter what I said, I couldn't convince him I was legitimately selling raffle tickets. It wasn't until I mentioned your name that he moved out of my way."

I arched a brow. "Are you legitimately selling raffle tickets?"

She glanced over her shoulder, then hurried to the table. "You told me I couldn't take anyone's purse, so I decided to get inventive to make some money."

My heart gave an unhappy stutter. "Gran! That's still stealing. You're running a fake raffle. That's a crime. Were you going to keep the money people gave you for those tickets? Is there even a prize?"

She looked away and played with a cookie cutter on the counter. "I could always rustle up a bottle of wine. Would that do as a prize?"

"You're scamming people. That's wrong." I puffed out a breath. "Did you tell Campbell that we're related? As soon as he knows who you are, he'll dig into your background."

"I kept my mouth shut. I know his type. Always so quick to jump to assumptions."

"He is, and he regularly does. Campbell likes to see the worst in people."

"Don't worry. I won't muddy your name by letting him know you're my granddaughter."

I set my icing bag down. I felt terrible for hiding our connection. I wanted to be proud of my gran and tell everyone about her, but, well, people were so quick to judge.

She patted the back of my hand. "Stop frowning or you'll get wrinkles. I didn't mean to cause any trouble. I wanted to get some money so I could buy us something delicious for dinner. I don't want you to see me as a burden."

"You're not! I love having you here. But, please, stop tricking people out of money."

She heaved out a sigh. "Maybe I should take up Betsy's offer of the cleaning job at the castle."

"No! I don't think you'd enjoy that."

Her expression was shrewd. "I know what you're thinking. The castle is full of treasures, and I might decide to walk off with a few."

I ducked my head. The thought had crossed my mind.

"You don't have to explain. And of course, if they did background checks, they'd find out that I'd just gotten out. Not that it matters. I can't see myself on my hands and knees scrubbing the floor tiles. I've always seen myself in a more glamorous occupation, something that involves wearing diamonds and drinking a lot of champagne."

"I want to believe you've changed. But the purses, and now this fake raffle ..." A weight settled on my shoulders. I wouldn't turn my back on her, she was family.

"I'm too old to change. And I don't want to. I don't want the cleaning job. The Audley's are safe from me. However, some of their antique vases may not be." She waggled her eyebrows.

I hushed her and looked around to make sure no one had overheard. "Don't even joke about that. If a member of Campbell's security team hears you, you'll be in trouble."

"Mr. Humor Bypass can jump off a cliff for all I care." She grabbed my arm. "I hope you're not sweet on him."

I almost dropped my icing bag. "I can promise you, Campbell isn't my type."

"You may be his. He looks at you in a strange way."

"Because he most likely wants to throttle me. When I get involved in the castle mysteries, he always tries to keep me out of the way. He usually fails."

She chuckled. "I can imagine he'd hate that, being pestered by a slip of a thing. Although with all these murders and dark deeds, you need to keep safe."

I deliberately hadn't mentioned my recent near miss involving my arm and a sharp butter knife. It would only make Gran worry. "I'm always careful. You have nothing to be concerned about."

"You're my favorite granddaughter. I need to worry."

"I'm your only granddaughter."

"Which makes you even more precious. I'd hate to think of you getting in trouble."

"Like you, you mean?" I bit my lip. Those words had come out harsher than I'd planned, but I was angry with Gran.

She waved the words away. "You're a hundred times better than me."

"Not true. You're amazing. You went through a really rough time with—"

"No! We don't say his name. I'm responsible for my own actions."

"But if he hadn't taken your money, you wouldn't be in this situation."

She pursed her lips. "This isn't open for debate. I make my own way in the world. I was the foolish one who allowed my head to be turned by a handsome man. I've learned my lesson from that. Men hold no power over me. I won't fall for that again."

"I'm sure you won't. And if you're struggling to get enough money, I'd be happy to give you some. I've got a little in savings. It's not really doing anything, and I'm not even sure what I'm saving it for."

Granny Molly shook her head. "I'm not taking money from you. I feel bad enough that I'm staying in your apartment. That's why I planned to cook tonight. I want you to know how much I appreciate you. You keep your money. I'll figure things out."

I gave her a huge hug. "What are you going to do with the raffle prize money you've taken? You know you can't keep it."

She wrapped her arms around me. "Are you sure I can't? Just this once? I've made plenty. We can dine on steak tonight if you'd like."

"No steak. There are always leftovers in the kitchen. I'll bring those back tonight."

She sighed and kissed my cheek. "I did see a leaflet for a local animal shelter. I could donate the money to them. That way, my bad deed is canceled out because I'm doing something good with the cash."

"I'm not sure the police would agree. Could you return the money to the people who bought the tickets?"

"Absolutely not. That would get me arrested. No, I'll do that. Give the unloved animals a treat." She stepped back and her gaze ran around the kitchen. "Now, what can I do to help in here?"

"Nothing. Chef Heston is strict. In fact, I'm surprised he hasn't come over and yelled because I've got a guest here while I'm working."

"If he yells at me, I'll yell right back. Shouting doesn't get you anywhere."

"It does with Chef Heston. But he's amazing with the food he creates. I've learned a lot from him."

"Hopefully you haven't learned the art of shouting to get your own way."

I laughed before taking a quick look around. "Definitely not. But since he must be out in the café or doing something for the family, why don't you help with the wedding cake. I need to put the finishing touches to it before it goes out on the display table. Do you remember how to make spun sugar?"

"Of course. In case you've forgotten, I taught you how to do that."

I tilted my head. "That's not the way I remember it. You set light to the saucepan on the one occasion you showed me how to make spun sugar."

She snorted a disbelieving laugh. "Then there's something wrong with your memory."

"How about I whip up the mix and you drizzle it over the top of the cake?"

"Only if you're sure I won't mess it up." She crossed her arms over her chest.

"I trust you." And I did. I knew she'd never do anything to harm me.

She winked at me. "Then let's get decorating."

An hour later, I stood back and admired my medieval wedding cake. The five layers were covered in white icing, with a forest theme of decoration framing each base using edible strands of colored icing and sugar. Edible berries had been frosted and iced, before being eased among the foliage. On the top tier of the cake sat a tiny edible replica of the family crest, two swords crossing in front of a fist clad in armor. It was covered in a thin cloud of spun sugar.

"It's very Game of Thrones," Gran said.

"It's not too much?"

She put an arm around my shoulders. "It's perfect. That's a real talent you've got. You worked so hard to get your qualifications. I'm thrilled you're putting them to good use."

"Who is this woman?" Chef Heston stalked over and glared at Granny Molly.

I glanced at her. I was sick of hiding our relationship. "This is my gran. She's staying with me for a while. She's come to see the cake I made. In fact, she helped me with the spun sugar. I learned some of my baking techniques from her when I was growing up."

Chef Heston's eyes narrowed. "She shouldn't be in here."

"That's no way to welcome someone." Granny Molly held her hand out, and Chef Heston reluctantly shook it. "That's better. Manners make a man."

He grunted, his attention switching to the cake. "Isn't it time that went out into the marquee?"

"I was about to do that. Gran, would you help me?"

Chef Heston opened his mouth, then snapped his jaw shut and shook his head. "Just hurry up. The Duke and Duchess will be out soon to have a final look around the fair. They'll expect to see the cake on display."

Granny Molly sucked in a breath as if she was about to hurl insults at Chef Heston. I grabbed her arm and squeezed, giving her a warning look.

She pressed her lips together, but frowned at Chef Heston's back as he walked away. "That one needs a good spanking."

I suppressed a laugh. "I'll suggest that to him the next time he's yelling, shall I?"

"I don't care how good a chef he is, your cake is incredible, and he didn't even give you a single compliment."

"He's busy. And he gets stressed easily. He shows his appreciation in other ways."

"Hopefully by giving you a big fat pay rise."

I nodded. It wasn't unusual to find a bonus in my pay packet at the end of the month when I'd worked hard on a project. "Let's get the cake on the trolley and over to the marquee."

Gran helped me lift the cake, and we wheeled it slowly outside. It took center stage on the Audley Castle display, and it wasn't long before a small crowd had formed, commenting on the design and how beautiful it was.

I glowed under their praise. All the hard work had been worth it.

"What have we got here?" Bruce Osman strolled over and peered at the cake. "That's an unusual design. I half expect to see a dragon poking its head out the middle."

"Holly made it," Granny Molly said, a proud expression on her face. "She's ever so clever."

Bruce shrugged. "I don't know much about cake, but I know plenty about wine."

"I like wine as well as cake," Granny Molly said, her eyes sparkling.

He turned a huge smile on her. "A woman of your beauty must have tasted a bounty of vintage delights."

She grinned. "Naturally. Do you have something to offer me?"

I suppressed a groan. How could Gran think Bruce was charming?

"Let me tempt you to a glass of Claret, compliments of Osman Vineyard," Bruce said.

Gran fluttered her lashes. "I wouldn't say no. What do you think, Holly? You must be in need of some refreshment after all your hard work."

"Nothing for me." My attention was drawn to a display that read 'Zoe Rossini, Wedding Planner to the Stars.'

I'd been distracted with my work in the kitchen, but I needed to get back to interviewing suspects. Whoever had poisoned Connie was most likely still lurking around this wedding fair.

"I'm going to sample some of this handsome man's wine," Gran said.

"You're too kind, Mrs. ..."

"Ms. I'm not married. You may call me Molly."

"Well, charming Molly, let me show you my goods."

"Behave yourself," I muttered to her.

She chuckled. "I always do. I'll see you later, back at the apartment." Gran sashayed away, her hand clasping Bruce's arm.

I shook my head. She still had a weakness for smooth talking men, no matter what she told me.

I did a final check of the cake, then headed over to speak to Zoe Rossini. Perhaps she'd be able to shed some light on what happened to Connie and who wanted her dead.

Chapter 16

"When's your special day?" Zoe was slim, pretty, with long blonde curls styled around her heart-shaped face. She held out a tray of love heart chocolates.

"My special day?" I peered at her.

"Your wedding day." She giggled as she lowered the tray. "Some brides plan three years in advance."

"Oh! No, I'm not getting married."

She tilted her head. "You're a bridesmaid? Doing some research for the bride to be?"

"Not exactly. I'm here about Connie Barber. Do you know what happened to her?"

Zoe's expression dropped and her eyes glistened. "Of course. You were friends? I don't think we've met before. Connie and I lost contact a while back."

"I met Connie just before she died. I'm sort of working with the castle security. We have some concerns about what happened to her."

Her full bottom lip jutted out. "I heard a rumor her death wasn't an accident. It's so terrible. We had our problems, but I thought we'd patch things up, eventually. We'd been friends for years. We started Florally Forever together when we were barely out of our teens."

"You went to school together?"

She sighed and straightened the leaflets on display. "That's right. Connie came to my rescue one day when I was being picked on. This mean girl was pulling my hair and threatening to push me over. Connie stopped her by throwing the bully's lunch bag in a bush. I figured we'd be friends for life."

"What changed?"

"The business took off."

I nodded. "I heard from one of the other florists that you'd had a few problems. Do you mind me asking what happened?"

Zoe fluffed out her hair. "I try not to be bitter about it. Connie was the brains of the operation. I was definitely the looks."

"I'm sure that's not true."

Her blue eyes tightened. "You're saying I'm not pretty?"

"I, um, no. I mean, you're very pretty."

"Thanks. It's important to look your best." Her gaze ran over me. "Is that flour on your pants?"

I looked down and dusted off the white flour coating my legs. "It's an occupational hazard."

"What are you doing covered in flour if you work in security?"

"Oh! It's not flour. It's ... fingerprint powder. Yes, we use it to dust for fingerprints."

"I've seen that on TV programs. I thought it was just a thing they did to make it look exciting. You really do that?"

"We all have unique fingerprints. If you get a match on the database, you can catch a criminal if you find their prints at a crime scene."

Her eyes widened. "Science is amazing and goes completely over my head. I'll stick to wedding planning. I make my own chocolates as well. Not to sell, just to give out to customers. That's how I was able to sneak a spot in the food and drink marquee. It's a lot more fun in here, and less competition from the other wedding planners. Some of those women are ruthless when it comes to stealing customers."

"So I've been hearing. When you and Connie parted ways, why didn't you start another business selling flowers?"

"The flowers are so pretty, but I have allergies. And although I love getting flowers, I don't like the runny nose and red eyes. When I worked with Connie, she handled the flowers, the books, the admin, and most of the business side of things. I did the promotion. Connie had a real eye for putting together stunning bouquets."

"It sounds like she was busy."

"Connie was always run off her feet. I'd always tell her not to stress. Things always sort themselves out in the end." She smiled and inspected her perfect pink nails.

I was seeing why Connie decided to stop working with Zoe. "Why did the success of Florally Forever change things between you?"

Zoe sighed. "I'm only saying this because it's the truth. My mom always told me never to lie. Connie cheated me."

"What did she do?"

She looked around. "I shouldn't say. It's not nice to speak ill of the dead."

"If it's the truth, there's no harm in talking about it."

"I suppose so." She twirled a strand of hair around one finger. "I lost my half of the business to her."

"Lost?"

"Connie tricked me out of it."

"You must have been angry about that."

"For a while, I was spitting mad. I wanted to slap her. No, I wanted to pull out her hair extensions, although she didn't wear those. I wanted to slash her favorite designer suit. She ruined things between us."

Zoe had a vicious side to her. A side that could have come out when she decided to poison Connie. "I'd be interested to know how she tricked you."

"I signed over the business without realizing what I was doing. One evening, we had a few drinks and were chatting about the next steps. She pulled out some paperwork and said I needed to sign it. I never questioned her. As I said, she was the smart one. I signed without thinking. The next thing I discovered, Connie had deposited some money in my account and left a note telling me to be out by the end of the week. She fired me!"

"She bought you out of the business?"

"For a fraction of what it was worth based on future income."

"I thought you didn't know anything about business?"

"I can read how many zeros are at the end of a big number. And she took the name as well. I loved that name. Florally Forever was my idea, but Connie said you can't copyright an idea."

"Do customers associate Florally Forever with excellence?"

"It has one of the best reputations for stunning arrangements. And as mean as Connie was, I can't deny she had a talent for creating unique bouquets. Florally Forever was going places. Connie got greedy. She said I wasn't cost effective and was a liability. She told me I had no role in the company and outsourced the promotion and PR to a firm overseas. How can you put a price on a friendship?"

Connie's behavior was cut throat, no matter how much of a dead weight Zoe was. And it also gave Zoe an excellent reason for wanting Connie dead.

"Did you ever get involved with handling the plants and flowers?" I asked.

"Only when I had no choice. Sometimes we'd get busy, and I'd have to help out."

"You must have learned about plants while working with Connie."

"I know a bit. I sometimes picked up the flower orders. That was until I wrote off the delivery van. Connie always told me not to drive in my high heels, but what was I supposed to do? Heels make my legs look slimmer. After I damaged the van, she told me to stick to designing the posters."

"Did she ever teach you about dangerous plants?"

"Dangerous plants? Venus fly traps, that sort of thing?"

"No, I was thinking about plants that are toxic to people. The kind you don't put in a floral bouquet."

"I don't have a clue about those. Why do you ask?"

"The police are investigating the possibility that Connie was poisoned."

Zoe's eyes bugged. "With what?"

"A toxin found in plants."

She gasped. "No, I can't believe that. She was really poisoned?"

"It looks like it."

"Oh my gosh! Why? Do they know who did it?"

"Not yet. Can you think of anyone who wanted her dead?"

"You mean, besides me?" She giggled. "Sorry, I always say the stupidest things when I'm nervous. The police are absolutely sure it wasn't an accident?"

"It was murder."

"I've just got goose bumps." She rubbed her hands up and down her arms. "Have you spoken to Leanna?"

"Connie's assistant? I have."

Zoe arched her eyebrows. "If I were investigating this as a murder, I'd take a look at her."

"Leanna had a problem with Connie?"

"She must have done. Connie bullied Leanna. I saw her do it. She was always snapping at her and ordering her around. She used to do it to me when we worked together. I didn't like it. I was a bit worried about Leanna and asked her about it. She brushed it off and said it was nothing, but I wasn't so sure. She's so young. She would be easy to manipulate. I don't think Connie was paying her well, either."

"You think she was taking advantage of Leanna's eagerness to learn?"

"Connie was a shrewd businesswoman. She was always looking for ways to trim the fat. That's what she used to say. When she first told me that, I thought she was suggesting I needed to lose weight."

I kept my expression neutral. "Do you remember where you were when Connie's body was found?"

Zoe's gaze cut to Bruce, who was flirting outrageously with my gran. "I was with a … friend."

"Does your friend have a name?"

She giggled again. "He does. Bruce. He's so handsome, older than me, and runs his own business. He's the perfect guy."

"Bruce also had an interest in Connie, didn't he?"

The smile slipped from Zoe's face. "Not anymore he doesn't. We were sampling his sparkling wine when news got back to us that Connie was dead."

Which confirmed what Bruce had told me. "Did you and Connie always attend the same wedding fairs?"

"Yes, most of the time. Why do you ask?"

"It must have been difficult seeing her after everything that happened between you. Did you ever reach out to her?

Try to make up?" My gaze went to her homemade chocolates. "Maybe you gave her some of your candy?"

"Nope. She wasn't interested in making up." Zoe shifted from foot to foot. "I often felt uncomfortable, but we'd been doing the circuit for years. I wasn't going to stop attending the lucrative fairs because she'd be there giving me those annoying little smirks and undercutting the competition."

A strangled, high-pitched female yell had me whirling around. Campbell and one of his security team, Kace, were racing across the marquee.

My eyes widened. They were chasing Tina. How was she even here?

Tina screamed again and raised her arm.

My stomach did a flip flop, and everything faded. All I could see was the can of gasoline in Tina's hand. She was pouring a line of it behind her.

Zoe shrieked and ducked behind her counter. "I thought she'd been banned from the wedding fair."

I winced as Campbell tackled Tina to the ground. She face-planted hard, the can of gasoline flying out of her hand.

Kace picked it up, standing beside her as Campbell pinned her down.

"You know Tina?" I asked Zoe.

She stood slowly, her wide-eyed gaze on the action. "Sadly, I do. She was always harassing Connie. Mind you, Connie was sleeping with her husband, so I don't blame her."

Tina screeched, drawing my attention back to her. "Let me go."

"Calm down," Campbell said.

Tina twisted in his grip, but she wasn't making any progress in getting away.

"Stay here," I said to Zoe. I raced over to Campbell. "What happened? I thought Tina was in custody."

He glanced up at me and rolled his eyes. "Trust you to see this."

"You let her go?"

"It looks like it. I couldn't hold her without evidence." Campbell adjusted his grip on Tina's arm. "But I made a mistake by setting her loose."

"I'm the one who made the mistake," Tina said. "I'm glad Connie is dead. She was a man-stealing witch. I want to shake the hand of whoever killed her."

"Wasn't it you?" I asked.

"Holly! Not now," Campbell said.

"I wish it had been me." Tina twisted her head and stared up at me. "It was probably another cheated-on wife who snapped."

"Tina Kennon, I'm arresting you, again, for the attempted destruction of public property, attempted arson, and attempted manslaughter."

Tina flipped up and down on her stomach. "Get off me! Connie had no morals. She trod over everyone to get what she wanted. I was doing the world a favor by going after her."

"That sounds like a confession," Campbell said.

"Get lost." Tina snarled. "You aren't the police. You can't hold me. This is assault."

"Wrong. I can. You fall under the rules of Audley Castle law."

"This is a joke. Let. Me. Go!"

Campbell didn't budge as Tina continued to squirm and yell insults.

"It takes two to tango." Zoe appeared by my elbow and peered down at Tina. "Your husband could have said no when Connie made a play for him."

Tina shrieked again. "Shove off, Barbie. I don't know why you always defend Connie. She dumped you like a mold-covered sponge once you got in her way. And I bet you covered for her when she was off with my guy. You were always simpering around, bowing to her demands like she was the bloomin' Queen of England."

Zoe's head jerked back. "I didn't! If you weren't able to keep hold of your man, then that's your problem. You should try a makeover, sort out that frizzy hair and pluck those hideous eyebrows. They make you look masculine."

"Holly, I really don't need this." Campbell gestured at Zoe. "I'm trying to keep a lid on this situation before this place goes up in flames."

I had a dozen questions to ask, but there was a growing crowd in the marquee looking to see what was going on.

I caught hold of Zoe's elbow. "We should get out of here. Let the security team do their job."

Zoe glared down at Tina before turning and walking away with me. "Forget what I said about Leanna, Tina's the real problem. Although I wasn't involved in Florally Forever when she started coming around, I knew she was making things difficult. I saw Connie and Tina go toe-to-toe several times. I asked Connie what was going on, but she wouldn't confide in me. Not that it mattered. Tina yelled loudly enough so we could all hear about the cheating."

"And it looks like she's not done with her revenge, even though Connie's dead. She must want to destroy everything she had." The smell of gasoline was strong in the air.

Zoe looked around. "She's lost her mind. Connie's display isn't even in here. Tina had the wrong marquee. I hope the police lock her up and throw away the key."

We stood and watched as Campbell hustled Tina away. Kace dealt with the gasoline spill, blocking it off so no one walked through it.

My mind flipped over what just happened. Tina was on a single track mission to destroy everything Connie had. Could she have found a way to poison her? Maybe she'd sent her food laced with ragwort. It would have been difficult, but not impossible. She was hell-bent on ruining everything Connie had built up, no matter the consequences.

"Are you okay?" Zoe asked. "You look a bit ... constipated."

I choked out a laugh. "This is my thinking face. I'm fine."

"This has certainly been an eventful wedding fair," Zoe said. "I'll be glad when it's over. Are you going to interview Tina now she's been arrested? Is that a part of your job, too?"

I wished it was. "I'll leave that to Campbell. He's got ways to make people talk."

"Maybe now Tina's back with the police, things can return to normal. Connie could be a right cow, but she didn't deserve to be poisoned by her own flowers." Zoe glanced over at her display. "If you'll excuse me, I've got customers waiting." She hurried away.

I walked over to the spilled gasoline and stared at it. Had I made this too complicated? Tina had every reason for coming after Connie. Maybe I was just missing a piece of the puzzle when it came to Tina. This was a revenge killing because of her ruined marriage.

I sighed as I walked out of the marquee. I needed to figure out how Tina had done it, then life at Audley Castle really could get back to normal.

Chapter 17

"I'd have been terrified, trapped in a marquee with an insane woman waving around some gasoline. You're lucky she didn't light a match." Alice strolled along beside me as I took Meatball for his usual morning walk the next day.

"I expect that was her next move," I said.

"And it sounds like Campbell was terribly brave tackling her."

"He was a real hero," I said.

She sighed. "Yes, he really is."

I chuckled and shook my head. I'd just finished updating Alice about my discoveries in Connie's murder. "Even though I was planning to speak to all the suspects again, Tina must be involved. Everything is pointing at her." Even as I said those words, I didn't believe them.

"Hmmm, I'm not so sure. I've been speaking to Granny about the suspects. She's had some ideas."

"Please say it was a useful premonition. Or a clue to find out how Tina killed Connie."

"No clues or premonitions about murder. And her predictions are still all about your wedding. It's so frustrating. I want her to discover who my Prince Charming will be, then I can allow him to whisk me off my feet." Alice giggled. "Wouldn't that be wonderful? Anyway, neither of us are convinced it was Tina who poisoned Connie."

"Even though the evidence guides us to her, I'm not sure either."

"Maybe Tina worked in a café that Connie used to visit," Alice said. "She could have dosed her morning latte."

I shook my head. "No, that wouldn't work. Connie traveled around the country most of the year for the wedding fairs. Tina wouldn't have been able to follow her. Maybe she's more devious than I realized. Tina kept confronting Connie at the fairs. That meant she knew her movements. Maybe she laced the food with ragwort at the other wedding fairs. After all, suppliers give out loads of free samples."

"If she'd done that, wouldn't more people have gotten sick?" Alice asked.

"Not necessarily. I've done more investigation into ragwort. Small doses don't do you harm. And it's such a bitter tasting plant, that if you ate some, you'd probably spit it out."

"How come Connie didn't do that? Surely, if it's that nasty tasting, she wouldn't have eaten any, let alone regular doses every day."

I tipped my head back and sighed. "I don't know. Maybe if you add enough sugar or spice, it could mask the bitterness. That's what cooks used to do with rotting meat, cover it in spices so pungent you couldn't detect the rot."

Alice's expression grew stern. "I hope you don't use that cooking method in the kitchen."

"I promise, you only get the freshest of produce."

"I'm relieved to hear it. It wasn't so long ago that my family employed a food taster before accepting the offerings from the kitchen."

"Because it wasn't good quality?"

"No. Because we had our fair share of people who wanted to poison us."

"I can't imagine anyone wanting to poison you."

"Oh, no. Everyone loves me. But a family member three hundred years ago was poisoned with hemlock juice in the same dining room we still eat in. It was most likely a shady character from the kitchen."

"There are no shady characters in the kitchen, anymore."

She nudged me with her elbow. "Chef Heston can be a bit grumpy."

"Alice! He's very good to you, especially when you make a last minute demand for afternoon tea."

"For which I'm eternally grateful. So, Tina. What are we going to do about her? I'm yet to be convinced she's a poisoner."

"I agree. From what I know about Tina, she's a woman more likely to act on impulse than plan something so stealthy."

"She's also a woman scorned, with a broken heart. Tina deserves justice," Alice said.

"Which gives her an amazing motive for murder. And Campbell is convinced Tina is behind this. He marched her out of the marquee yesterday, and I've yet to discover what happened to her."

"As much as I admire Campbell, you know he isn't always right about these things. Tina seems like too obvious a suspect to me."

"And a flawed suspect, given her impetuous behavior. Maybe the real killer figured we'd all look at Tina because she's been so passionate in her pursuit of revenge. Tina's been set up to take the fall."

"From what you told me, she did have plans to murder Connie. She's not completely innocent."

"Yes, but not with poison. Whoever wanted Connie dead, fed her ragwort over a long time period. They knew what they were doing and were willing to bide their time to make sure she suffered."

Alice shuddered and rubbed her arms. "Tina isn't the cold, calculating type. She wanted everything Connie owned to go up in a dramatic blaze to prove her point. I think you're on the right track going to speak to the remaining suspects again."

"There's someone I do want to speak to. Leanna, Connie's assistant. When I was talking to Zoe yesterday, she said Connie treated her badly. She was bullying her and taking advantage of the fact she was so new to the world of weddings."

"There you go, then. We'll keep looking around and make some progress in finding the real killer. Campbell can deal with the hothead with the gasoline."

"I want to speak to Campbell, too, and see what Tina told him."

"I saw him briefly this morning, but he was on his way out. He's probably with the police. You'll have to wait if you want to talk to him."

My belly rumbled. "No matter. I need to finish Meatball's walk and then have some breakfast."

Alice grinned. "That sounds like the perfect idea. I'll join you for my second breakfast."

I hesitated. Granny Molly was still staying with me, and I'd yet to reveal to Alice who she was. "Another time. I was just going to grab something quick and head into work."

"I was looking forward to your scones. That's very disappointing news." Her eyes narrowed, and she grinned wickedly. "I could always order you to have breakfast with me."

"You'd better not. Chef Heston is still growling at me because I let my—" I stopped before I blurted out that Gran had been in the kitchen. "I burned some blueberry blast muffins."

"That's not like you. What a terrible waste. Oh well, I don't want you to get in trouble. We're definitely having breakfast together soon. I want to talk to you about the plogging event. I've got some ideas to make it extra special."

"Tell me now." I'd barely given my event any thought, I'd been so involved with Connie's murder.

"Fancy dress. We dress up and make it more fun." Alice spread her arms out wide. "I'm thinking an epic historical theme to fit with the castle."

"Sure you are. You just want to force Campbell into a knight in shining armor outfit so you can swoon over him."

"The thought hadn't crossed my mind." She grinned at me. "He would look handsome as a gallant knight. And he knows how to ride. I've been out with him several times. He rides the stallion."

"Of course he does." I slid her a sideways glance. "Alice, are you ever going to get over your obsession with him? How are you supposed to find a man to marry if you're so hung up on Campbell?"

"I'm not hung up on him. I simply … appreciate his hard work and dedication to me."

"As your head of security, that's what he's supposed to do. But do you think he likes you as in 'I want to walk with this cute girl under a starry night and whisper sweet nothings in her ear' kind of way?"

"Oooh! Wouldn't that be fun?"

"Alice! Campbell is a serious, headstrong alpha male. And sometimes, he can be a big jerk."

"He also has a soft side. He likes me, I'm sure of it."

I shook my head. "He likes his big pay check and the fact he gets to strut around this castle like he owns it."

"Oh! Do you really think that's all it is?" She kicked a stone.

I hated to burst her bubble, but she couldn't think anything would ever go on between them. "Has he ever said anything to suggest he likes you?"

"Lots of things. He's always telling me he needs to look out for me and he's here to protect me."

"Because that's his job." I softened my words as much as I could.

"If that's the case, I can have him sacked. Then he'd be free to declare his feelings. Would that work?"

"Taking a man's job from him is probably the worst thing you can do if you want him to fall in love with you," I said. "How about you go on a few dates with other men? Get him out of your system. I'm sure there are lots of lovely guys out there for you."

"There aren't. At least not the ones my parents think are suitable. No, the plogging event is a perfect opportunity to get to know Campbell better. He won't be working, so we can share an enjoyable activity together."

He may not officially be working, but Campbell would be on high alert if Alice was joining in the plogging, but there was no dissuading her from this.

"I'll put the word out about the fancy dress element," Alice said, seeming happy now she'd figured out how to spend time with Campbell. "What will you go as?"

"I won't have time to come up with an outfit," I said. "I'm focusing on Connie's murder, and I'll have a mountain of baking to get through today." Plus, I had my gran to keep an eye on.

"That's fine. I'll find something for you to wear."

"Noooo! I'll wear my usual workout clothes. And since I'm the organizer, I need to be easy to spot if there are any questions. If I'm hiding in a costume, it could create problems for people taking part. What if someone gets injured?"

"Nonsense. We all have to make an effort, especially you, since you're in charge."

A shiver of worry ran through me. Alice was known for her grand gestures. And when it came to choosing fancy dress costumes, she'd pull out all the stops. I could end up as Marie Antoinette, trying to run with a huge wig on my head and a giant skirt.

I checked the time. "I have to get to work. Let's meet up later once I've spoken to Leanna."

"Great. And I'll get to work on our costumes."

I grabbed her arm. "Don't go wild. Something simple and easy to run in is all I need."

She giggled. "You know me, I like to make an effort."

I repressed a grimace. We said our goodbyes, and I hurried away with Meatball. Maybe I should cancel the plogging. I wasn't sure what I was getting myself into now Alice was involved, but I knew I'd end up looking foolish once she'd dressed me.

Meatball woofed at me and wagged his tail.

"Don't think you're getting out of being dressed up, either. Alice will probably order you a tiger costume. Or maybe a pink tutu and a tiara."

"Woof!" He shook himself.

"Yes, that's exactly how I feel."

"I'm just taking my lunch break, Chef." I pulled off my apron and headed to the door.

"We're getting low on blueberry blast muffins," he said, his focus on the Bakewell tart in front of him.

I pointed to the counter where two dozen muffins sat cooling. "I'm already on it. Those will be ready to go in ten minutes."

He glanced at the muffins and jerked his head toward the door. "Get out of here."

Getting any food for myself would have to wait. I was on a mission. I hurried over to the marquee and straight to Connie's flower stand.

I slowed, my brow lowering. Granny Molly was standing behind the display chatting to a couple. I waited for them to go before heading over. "What are you up to?"

She grinned. "Looking after this. The young girl who was here said she needed a break and would I mind taking care of it. I've been wandering around the wedding fair for a couple of hours and we got chatting earlier. She seems nice, and I had nothing better to do, so I was happy to help."

"What do you get out of it?"

"Leanna promised to bring me some lunch. I figured it was a good deal. Although she's been gone a while. The queues must be long in the food tent."

I hung around with Gran and chatted for a few minutes, waiting for Leanna to get back.

"I wish she'd hurry up," Granny Molly said. "I'm getting hungry. I'll scare away potential customers if my stomach keeps growling like this."

"How long has she been gone?"

"Half an hour," Gran said.

My gaze flicked around the stand. "Did she take anything with her?"

"She had a bag and her coat. She left her laptop behind, though."

"How did she seem? Was she on edge about anything?" A swirl of nerves shot through me. Was Leanna making a run for it?

"She seemed fine. Maybe a little jumpy. She wouldn't stand still and kept walking around and talking too fast. I figured she was still in shock after what happened to her boss."

I took a step away from the stand. "Did Leanna talk to anyone before she left?"

"Not that I saw. Why all the questions about her?" Gran's eyes widened. "You don't think she had anything to do with what happened to Connie?"

"That's what I wanted to chat to her about. Did you see which way she went?" I was already scanning the crowd, hoping to catch a glimpse of Leanna returning.

"She headed over to the parking lot." Granny Molly shook her head. "She's a child. She wouldn't hurt anybody."

"Maybe she would if they were bullying her. You stay here, Gran. I'm going to see if I can find her." I dashed out of the marquee and was just making my way toward the parking lot when a white van passed me. On the side of it was a logo for Connie's business. Leanna was sitting in the driver's seat.

My heart thudded. She *was* making a run for it. Why would she do that if she was innocent?

I ran alongside the van and banged on the side of it. It stopped, and I raced to the driver's window.

Leanna stared at me. She wound down the window an inch. "Holly? What do you want? I'm in a hurry."

"I need to talk to you. Where are you going?"

"I, well, yes. I need to be somewhere."

"You're coming back? You can't leave my gran on your stand all day."

"I have to go." She shut the window, stamped on the gas, and the van lurched forward.

I tried to keep up with her, but she quickly pulled away.

I spotted a delivery bike propped against the wall of the castle. I grabbed it and jumped on, pedaling furiously in an attempt to keep up with Leanna. If she'd killed Connie, she needed to come clean.

The private road leading out of the castle curved in a large loop around the front of the building. At the end of the lane, you had the option to turn left, which took you into a delivery area, or right, which directed you out of the castle. I knew exactly which way Leanna would go.

I could catch up with her if I took a shortcut through the small copse of trees to my right.

I lifted off the saddle as I headed off the even surface of the road and over the bumpy grass. I kept pedaling as fast as I could. I'd be able to cut off a huge corner of the route if I went through the trees, and with a bit of luck would come out just in front of Leanna.

My breath rasped out of me and my muscles burned as I flew across the grass and into the trees.

Leanna couldn't get away. Now I knew Connie had bullied her, it gave her a great motive for wanting her dead. And she'd have had ample opportunity to slip ragwort into Connie's food. Since they worked together every day, it would have been easy to do, and Connie would have trusted her.

I burst out of the trees and almost cheered when the van was just making the right turn, heading away from the castle. I shot back onto the road and cycled toward the van.

Leanna waved at me to get out of the way as she drew nearer.

I shook my head and dug in. She'd stop. She wouldn't run me over. She couldn't be that desperate, could she?

As we drew nearer, a buzzing sounded in my head. Was that my subconscious screaming at me to stop being an idiot and get out of the way of the oncoming vehicle before it ran me over?

No, Leanna knew me. She wouldn't hurt me. She wouldn't want another death on her conscience. I had to believe that. Still, it didn't look like she was stopping, and my legs began to shake.

I swung one leg over the bike saddle, balanced on a pedal, and at the last second, let go of the bike and jumped to the side. I tumbled onto the grass and flipped several times, before landing on my back.

There was a crunch of metal grinding against metal and tires screeched.

I pulled myself onto my knees and gasped in a breath. The bike was mangled under the van's front tires. If I'd timed that wrong, that would have been me all mangled and squished.

Leanna jumped out and ran around to the front of the van. "What did you do that for?"

I staggered to my feet and hurried over. "I had to stop you. Why were you running?"

Her panicked gaze went back to the bike. "I wasn't running."

"Leanna, you just tried to run me over. It has to be something serious for you to do that."

"I ... I had to get away." Her top lip beaded with sweat and her breathing was shallow. "You don't understand. I had no choice."

"You always have a choice."

She gestured at the van. "Thanks to you, I have no choice now."

"You should have stopped to talk to me." I sucked in another breath. I was trying hard not to think about how close to death I'd just been. "Leanna, I know Connie didn't treat you well."

Her head shot around. "Who said that?"

"That's not important. Is it true?"

"I've already told you that I was glad she took me on. I had no experience when I joined Connie's company. I've learned a lot." Her words whooshed out on a breath. "Now, I really have to go."

"I expect you learned that it's no fun to be mistreated by your boss."

She was silent for several long, thudding heartbeats. "Connie never mistreated me."

"Are you sure? Did she yell at you? Tell you that you were stupid? Make you feel bad about things you'd done?"

Leanna looked around. She twisted her hands in front of her. "Sometimes. She always needed things done just so. I tried my best, but it wasn't always good enough. I was learning to get better."

"Connie was wrong to treat you like that. That's bullying."

Leanna let out a shaky sigh. "I thought that sort of thing stopped in the playground. I got picked on at school, too. It brought back bad memories when she snapped at me."

"I'm not surprised. That was a horrible thing to go through."

She gulped. "Connie was a horrible boss. Sometimes, she treated me like a servant. I was always running around after her. And she'd call me at all hours of the day and night demanding I do things at a moment's notice. I didn't want to lose my job and get a bad reference from her, so I agreed to everything, but I was miserable. Are all bosses like that?"

"Not all of them. There are good ones." I briefly considered Chef Heston. He had a bad habit of yelling, but there was a good heart buried beneath his surliness, and I'd never once seen him bully anyone.

Leanna slumped against the van. "I didn't realize how much stress I was under until Connie died. A weight vanished. I was no longer scared to open my mouth for fear of being told off. I'd gotten so used to her rants that it became normal. I wish I could be sad she's dead, but I'm not. Even though I'm out of a job and won't get paid for working this fair, I don't care. I feel free."

"Leanna, you know I have to ask this. Did you kill Connie because of the way she treated you?"

She shook her head vigorously. "Absolutely not. That's why I ran. People were starting to talk. I'd heard she was poisoned. I was around Connie all the time and always got her lunches and coffees. I could easily have poisoned her. That's what you're thinking, isn't it? That's why you chased me."

I nodded. "I'd understand if you couldn't take any more from her. I'm not saying killing Connie was right, but you were under a huge amount of pressure because of her mistreatment. If you confess, the judge will be lenient on you. You were under mental stress."

"But it wasn't me! I see how terrible this looks. I found the body. What's to say I didn't give her a dose of poison and dump her in the toilet?"

"Can no one vouch for your whereabouts just before Connie died?"

"No, I don't think anyone saw me. I went to the van to check stock. I was in the back for about five minutes trying to find a picture of a bouquet for a customer. Then I nipped to the toilet. That's when I found Connie at the same time as that cleaning lady."

"What have people been saying to make you think you're a suspect?"

"Zoe's been looking at me funny all morning. She said something about it always being the quiet ones. I asked her what she meant, but she giggled and walked off."

"And you thought she was talking about Connie's murder?"

"Of course! I knew what she meant. And it would only be a matter of time before the police came and took me away."

"Maybe not. They've arrested Tina again."

She shook her head. "I heard what she tried to do, but I've been thinking about it. It couldn't be her. If this poison was so slow acting, Tina would have needed to be around Connie for months, and they hated each other. Connie actively avoided her."

I bit the inside of my cheek. Leanna looked guilty. She had plenty of opportunity to commit the crime, and she had a good motive.

The sound of a roaring engine had me looking up. A black SUV cruised to a stop behind the van. Campbell climbed out and strode over.

His gaze ran over the mangled bike. "Is anyone hurt?"

"We're fine. How did you know I was out here?" I asked.

"You were spotted chasing someone," he said.

"Who saw me?"

He lifted a shoulder. "I have eyes everywhere. You'd be wise to remember that. Explain this." He gestured to the damaged van and Leanna.

I sent an apologetic look Leanna's way. I couldn't conceal this from Campbell. "I learned that Connie was bullying Leanna."

"She was, but I didn't kill her." Leanna stared at me with a horrified look in her eyes. "Connie could be an awful human being, and she was mean to almost everyone, but I was used to it. I'd planned to work for her for another six months and then move on."

Leanna looked genuinely terrified, her body shaking and her face sweaty.

A shiver of doubt ran through me. Could she be that good at hiding the truth?

"Why were you leaving the wedding fair?" Campbell asked her.

"As I was telling Holly, I got spooked. Zoe kept making comments about the police looking into Connie's murder. I don't have an alibi. It would be easy to assume that I didn't like her because of the way she treated me."

"What can you tell me about ragwort?" I asked Leanna.

"Why are you asking about that?" Campbell said.

I glanced at him. "That was the poison used to kill Connie."

He looked at me as if I'd taken leave of my senses. "No, it wasn't."

"It was! Connie was poisoned with a plant toxin. Betsy told me it was ragwort."

"And you believe everything Betsy tells you? Did she happen to have a drink in her hand when she was disclosing this vital piece of information that she somehow stumbled across?"

My jaw dropped, and I groaned. "She said she overheard …" It was probably best I didn't drop Betsy in it by revealing she'd been eavesdropping on Campbell's team.

"She overheard what? She'd better not be snooping into private conversations. I'll have her job if she is. That's a breach of security." Campbell glowered at me.

"It doesn't matter where she heard the information. The source was reliable," I said.

"No, it wasn't." Campbell turned to Leanna. "I have some questions for you. We can go to the local police station."

Leanna's bottom jaw trembled. "I can't help you. I didn't do this."

"Let's find out if that's true." He led her to the back passenger door of the SUV.

"Please, I'm not involved. I just want to get on with my life." Leanna shot a terrified look my way.

I was still reeling from the revelation that I'd gotten the method of murder so wrong. "Wait! Connie was poisoned with a toxic plant, wasn't she?" I hurried along beside Campbell and Leanna.

Campbell slid me a sharp look as he settled her in the SUV and closed the door. "Nope."

"But you said she had plant toxin in her system when the autopsy was done."

"She did."

I shook my head. "So what killed her if it wasn't that?"

He sucked air through his teeth, a smirk sliding across his face.

"Campbell! Don't make me threaten to set Princess Alice on you."

He snorted out a grunt. "You would as well."

"I'm desperate."

He raised a hand. "There was a mix up at the lab. They were short-staffed and muddled up the results."

"Then what was it? It was poison?"

"Of a sort. And she had plant toxins in her system, but that didn't kill her."

"A different poison did?"

His jaw muscles clenched. "Why do you need to know?"

"Because ..." I didn't, but I hated loose ends. "At least tell me how Connie ingested the poison. Was she given a large dose which killed her?"

He shrugged a shoulder. "You're the one who's always solving these puzzles. Why don't you figure it out?" He walked to the driver's side door.

I looked in at Leanna. Tears were streaming down her cheeks and her shoulders were hunched.

If I'd gotten the murder weapon so wrong, what else had I gotten wrong? Who was the real killer?

Chapter 18

"This will cheer you up." Alice held my hand as she led me up the east turret steps, Meatball racing ahead of us.

"The only thing that'll cheer me up is hiding under a duvet for a week and eating my bodyweight in cupcakes." Everything felt lost. I didn't know which way to turn after Campbell had taken Leanna away and revealed I'd gotten the poison wrong.

"Granny has ordered a feast from the kitchen. We're having six courses. That'll make anybody smile."

I did muster a tiny smile. I knew exactly what the kitchen had prepared for Lady Philippa. It would be delicious.

We headed through the door into Lady Philippa's rooms.

"Oh! I didn't know you were coming." My gran sat at the table with Lady Philippa, a large glass of red wine in one hand.

"I didn't want your … friend to feel left out." Alice gave me a pointed look. "She would have been on her own this evening, since you're dining with us. It only seemed right she come, too."

My mouth twisted to the side. From the tone of Alice's voice, she knew Gran was more than a friend.

Granny Molly placed down her glass. She stood and walked over to me. "You don't mind me being here, do you? I promise, I'll be on my best behavior."

"Of course I don't." I squeezed her arm. "I'm glad you're here."

I saw the curious expression on Alice and Lady Philippa's faces. It was time to come clean. "I'd like you both to meet my gran."

Alice gasped. "Holly! You never said that's who she was. Of course, now you're standing side-by-side, I see the family resemblance. What were you doing, hiding her from us?"

I glanced at my gran. "I wasn't exactly hiding her. It's —"

"My fault," Granny Molly said. "I'm shy when meeting new people. I wanted a few days to settle in and find my feet before Holly started showing me off."

Lady Philippa gave a quiet snort that suggested she didn't believe a word of it. "Well, you're all here now. And here comes the food. Let's get settled at the table. I want to hear all about this murder."

My low mood returned. Every time I dwelled on what happened to Connie, I got glum. I thought I'd figured it out when Leanna had tried to get away. Was I losing my touch?

The servers laid out the first course before leaving. It was a pink pepper watermelon and chevin salad with purple basil and pickled ginger.

"Your granddaughter has a wonderful way of figuring out the impossible," Lady Philippa said to Granny Molly. "She's an asset to you."

"I think so, too," Granny Molly said, a wide smile on her face. "Although all this news of her solving murders is worrying."

"She never told you about her adventures?" Alice asked.

"No, not a word until I arrived and discovered first-hand what she's been doing."

"I only kept quiet about it so you wouldn't be concerned," I said. "Most of the time, life here is very ordinary."

"If you call living in a castle ordinary," Granny Molly said, casting her gaze around the impressive circular turret, the windows draped with heavy brocade curtains, and the tapestries on the wall.

"That's true. But it's ordinary to us," Lady Philippa said. "Where do you live?"

Gran glanced at me. "I'm in between places. I'm thinking about trying somewhere new."

"If you don't mind the occasional murder, I can highly recommend Audley St. Mary," Alice said. "And you'd be close to Holly if you lived here. You could see each other every day."

"I'll add it to the list." Gran winked at me. "It would be great to see more of each other."

I smiled at her. "Yes, it would." I only had a small family. I should make more of an effort to see them.

"This is a delicious salad," Lady Philippa said.

"I'm looking forward to the dessert the most," Alice said. "It's lavender peach tarte tatin with honeycomb ice cream."

"Did you make the dessert, Holly?" Lady Philippa asked.

"I did. Chef Heston insisted," I said.

She gave an approving nod. "Excellent. You always make the best puddings."

I ate a couple of bites of my salad. It was tasty, but my thoughts were on a much darker subject.

"What's got you so down at the mouth?" Granny Molly tapped the back of my hand.

"I've gotten in a mess with this latest mystery," I said. "I jumped to conclusions about Tina and then Leanna, but now I'm not sure about either of them."

"Leanna was the girl who had me looking after her stand," Granny Molly said. "The one you chased after."

"You were assisting a killer?" Lady Philippa turned her gaze on Granny Molly.

"Only by accident," Gran said. "And she seemed like such a sweet girl. A bit on the nervous side, though. Now I know why."

"And she was really making a run for it?" Alice asked.

"She was. I managed to catch up with her. Then Campbell caught us and took her away," I said. "I haven't heard what happened since then."

"Why are you having doubts about Leanna being guilty? Her behavior suggests she was involved," Lady Philippa said.

"She was so distraught when I asked her if she'd killed Connie."

"Because she'd been caught," Alice said.

"I'm not so sure," I said.

"What about the crazy woman with the can of gasoline?" Granny Molly said.

"Tina. She was initially my prime suspect," I said. "But she's too obvious. It's as if the killer realized everyone would think it was her, so they could fly under the radar and get to Connie."

"From the accounts I've heard of that woman, she was unstable," Lady Philippa said.

"True, but we both have doubts about Tina being Connie's killer after learning more about her," Alice said.

I nodded. "She's too impulsive. Tina wouldn't be able to wait while she slowly poisoned Connie. She demonstrated her recklessness when she tried to burn down the marquee.

And she also wouldn't have had access to Connie to administer the poison."

We were all quiet for a moment as we ate our food.

"Anyone else on your suspect list?" Gran asked.

"There's Belinda Adler," I said. "She hated Connie. But she was on her computer ordering flowers when Connie died, and she seemed genuinely saddened by her murder."

"Could she have faked her alibi?" Lady Philippa asked.

"No, I checked her phone and laptop," I said. "She was definitely speaking to the flower wholesaler at the time of the murder."

"What about the boyfriend?" Alice asked.

"Bruce Osman?" I said.

"Is that the charming man who gave me all that free wine?" Gran asked.

"He's charming but prone to getting obsessed with the women he dates," I said. "At least, that's what happened with Connie."

She frowned. "Oh! And I was thinking I might bag myself a toy boy."

I raised my eyebrows at her, and she chuckled and clinked glasses with Lady Philippa.

"What about Zoe?" Alice asked.

"Zoe and Bruce alibi for each other," I said. "And when I spoke to Zoe, she was sad about what happened to her friend. I think she wanted to rekindle the friendship, but Connie wasn't interested. She was open about being angry because Connie cheated her, but she didn't want her dead."

"I know you have your doubts about Leanna, but she had the opportunity to poison Connie," Alice said. "They were together most days."

"I agree that it would have been simple for her to add poison to Connie's food, but she was terrified when Campbell caught up with her. I believed her when she said she was innocent. And Leanna had plans for the future.

Why ruin those when she was getting ready to move on and cut Connie out of her life?"

"She looks guilty because she ran," Lady Philippa said. "That was a foolish thing to do."

"She panicked. Zoe was making snide comments about what happened to Connie, and Leanna realized she could be in trouble. I don't think she thought it through. She was in self-preservation mode."

The servers cleared the plates and brought in the second course. It was butter baked sea bass with braised carrots, tomato jam, and baby spinach.

I waited until they left before continuing. "That's not the biggest problem. I got the murder weapon wrong."

"It wasn't plant poison?" Alice asked.

"It wasn't ragwort. And Campbell wouldn't reveal what it was. It's my own fault. I didn't look into it after Betsy revealed the news in the pub that night. She overheard the security team discussing ragwort, but maybe they were discussing different plant poisons that could have been used, and not the actual poison."

"But Connie was definitely poisoned?" Lady Philippa said.

"Yes, although I don't know what was used."

"It doesn't make much of a difference what kind of poison it was. It'll kill you in the end," Lady Philippa said.

"Maybe it does matter, though. It could be a rare plant poison," I said. "That would cut down the number of people who knew what it was and how to get access to it."

"There's a simple way to solve this." Lady Philippa gestured to the door. "Alice, instruct one of the servers to fetch Mr. Smith from his apartment."

"You know Ray?" I asked.

"I know all the castle staff. He's a delightful man and often talks to me about the roses when I'm looking at them."

"I've already spoken to Ray about plant poison," I said. "He was helpful. If anyone knows what the poison could be, it would be him. At least, he could give us other options."

Alice hurried off to ask a member of the serving team to summon Ray, and we continued with our delicious dinner.

"Actually, I have something that may help with this puzzle, as well." Gran placed her knife and fork down. "It's back at the apartment. I could go and get it."

"What is it?" I asked, thinking back to the purse she'd lifted from Tina. Had she snagged Leanna's purse, too?

"Any clue will help," Lady Philippa said. "Go grab it now. The third course won't be served for some time."

She flashed me a smile before leaving the room.

"Are you quite well?" Lady Philippa asked. "You look worried about something."

I was worried. Had Granny Molly been stealing again? "It's nothing."

She arched a brow. "It's definitely something. And it's not just about this curious poisoning."

I opened my mouth to speak, when Alice returned. "I told the staff to get Ray immediately. It's an emergency."

"The poor man will probably sprint here." Lady Philippa tutted.

"This is important. We have a killer to find." Alice sat at the table. "I like your gran, Holly. She's sweet."

"From what I've been hearing, she's led a colorful life," Lady Philippa said.

I jerked upright, every muscle tensing. "What has she told you?"

Her face gave nothing away. "Not much. But I get the impression she's a clever, resourceful woman. You must get your intellect from her."

I was relieved Gran hadn't been sharing her secrets of life behind bars. "I'm glad to have her back in my life."

"Where has she been all this time?" Alice asked.

"Oh! Nowhere special. She just gets … caught up in things, that's all. I sometimes don't hear from her for ages."

Lady Philippa arched an eyebrow again but didn't say anything.

My stomach flipped. Exactly what had Granny Molly told her?

We ate a little more dinner, but my appetite was gone. I hated keeping Gran's secret. Maybe I shouldn't.

There was a knock on the door, saving me from any more interrogation about Gran and her mysterious past.

"Come in," Lady Philippa said.

Ray appeared, his cap in his hand and his cheeks pink as if he'd run up the steps. "Lady Philippa, Princess Alice." He nodded at me. "Holly. I came as quickly as I could. Is there something I can help you with?"

"There is." Lady Philippa gestured to a chair. "Take a seat. Would you like some wine?"

"No, thank you. I was just making a hot cocoa when I got the message you needed to see me." He perched on the edge of the chair, looking ready to leap to his feet at any second.

Meatball bounded over, his tail wagging.

"Hello, boy. Good to see you." Ray plucked a biscuit from his pocket and fed it to him.

Horatio lumbered to his feet and stomped over, nudging Ray with his nose.

"You, too? You probably don't need anything else to eat." He looked at Lady Philippa. "No offense meant."

"Nonsense. That is one fat, greedy hound. Still, he'd probably like a biscuit if you have a spare one."

Ray swiftly fed Horatio a dog biscuit.

"We want to know more about plant poisons," Lady Philippa said.

Ray glanced at me. "Of course. You didn't get what you needed when we spoke?"

"I did. That was helpful. But I'm interested in another poison. It needs to be slow acting, make someone feel unwell, but still be able to function. It would also need to give them trouble with their stomach and problems with balance and coordination."

He scrubbed a hand across his chin. "There are a number of poisonous plants that could do that."

"Are any of them rare or exotic?" I asked.

"The most poisonous plants are usually the ones you find in your garden," Ray said. "There's foxglove. If you eat the leaves you get sick, your heart can slow, and you get chest pain."

"What about stomach pain? Connie was definitely having stomach problems."

"I reckon so," Ray said. "But most of the toxic plants aren't a problem unless you eat large amounts of the berries, stems, or get the berry juice all over your skin. The plant we were discussing the other day, ragwort, is more a problem for horses rather than humans. Sometimes they eat it because it grows in their paddocks. I was surprised when you asked about ragwort because it's so bitter. A lot of them are. If you eat them by mistake, you can taste the bitterness and know it's not good for you."

"Much like kale," Alice said. "That always tastes bitter to me, no matter how it's cooked."

"Kale is good for you. You're just fussy when it comes to your greens," I said.

She poked her tongue out at me. "If ragwort was added to Connie's food, she should have been able to taste it."

"It would have been hard to disguise," Ray said. "A hot chili sauce would probably mask the bitterness."

"And we're definitely looking for a plant poison?" Alice asked me.

"I … well, I assume so. Campbell told me ragwort wasn't the poison. Maybe I've got that wrong as well."

"Have you ladies formed a real murders club?" Ray asked, a smile on his face. "You're taking this death very seriously."

"I'm back." Granny Molly hurried through the door, a laptop case clutched in her hands. "Oh! We have company."

Ray stood and nodded. "Nice to meet you. I'm Ray Smith. Head Gardener for the castle."

"I'm Molly." Her cheeks flushed pink.

"Are you a member of the Audley family?" Ray asked. "Do I need to bow or call you princess?"

Granny Molly giggled. "Heavens, no. I'm no one special."

"If you don't mind me saying, you look very special to me. You have an elegant way about you. That's why I assumed you were a member of the family."

The flush on Granny Molly's cheeks grew, and I suppressed a smile. She always loved a sweet talking guy.

"That'll be all for now, Ray," Lady Philippa said. "Unless you have any more questions, Holly."

"No, not for now. Thanks, Ray. Maybe I'll come by tomorrow to pick your brains about plant poison some more if that's okay."

"Absolutely. I'll do whatever I can to help you ladies." He nodded, flashing my gran a brilliant smile, before leaving.

"What have you got there?" I asked as Gran settled back in her seat.

"Ray seemed nice." She ignored my question.

"He's very nice." I nodded at the laptop.

"Is he single?"

"I've never asked. Why?" I narrowed my eyes at her.

"Oh! Just asking for a friend." She smoothed her hands over her hair.

"So …" I gestured at the laptop.

Gran smiled slyly. "Leanna had a laptop she used for work. In her haste to get away, she left it behind." She pulled it out of the case and opened it. "I thought this might help us prove her innocence, or otherwise."

"How come you've got it?" My gut clenched and my mouth went dry. I almost didn't want to hear her response.

"I borrowed it. I don't have my own right now, and Leanna's not going to use it in her current situation. I thought it could be useful." She didn't meet my gaze as she spoke.

I grumbled under my breath. I'd have to have words with her about *borrowing* people's things, but not in front of Lady Philippa and Alice. "Let me take a look."

She placed it in the center of the table so we could all see. "I was looking through it earlier. Leanna takes a lot of pictures. She has folders full of them."

"She mentioned an interest in photography." I moved my plate to one side and scanned through the laptop files. I opened a file labeled *Audley Fair* and flicked through some pictures.

"She's taken pictures of you with Rupert." Alice leaned over to peer at the screen. "You look so sweet together."

Granny Molly nodded. "You make a great pair. It looks like you were at a real wedding."

I smiled, indulging in the briefest of fantasies that it had been a real wedding.

"I'll have to get a copy of these," Gran said. "You so rarely wear pretty dresses, Holly."

"I do. On special occasions."

"I'd like some, too," Lady Philippa said. "Even though it wasn't a real wedding, it would be nice to see one of my grandchildren standing at the altar. It seems Alice is dead set on not finding love."

"I would if I could," Alice said curtly.

"Look at that cute dog," Gran said. "Who's that little sweetie?"

"That was Connie's dog, Saffron. She may look sweet, but she's a bit of a grump." I flicked through more pictures. There were several of Saffron not looking happy at having her photo taken. Her ears were down and her tail was between her legs.

I moved on to some pictures of Connie holding Saffron. Misty stood beside her, a frown on her face as she focused on Saffron. I leaned closer to the screen, my breath hitching. In one of the photos, Misty was passing Connie a mug.

"I dismissed her," I whispered.

"Who are you talking about?" Alice looked at the screen. "Isn't that the dog whisperer lady?"

I nodded. "She couldn't … I mean, Misty was with me when Connie's body was found."

Alice's brow furrowed. "You're thinking she's involved? Why would the pet companion kill Connie? She paid her wages. She's out of a job now and has a dog to find a home for."

My heart pounded like I'd just spotted a freight train coming my way and was stuck on the track. "She had access to Connie's food and drink. This picture proves it. And she's been working with Connie for almost a year. Did she get the job so she could poison Connie?"

"Could she be another cheated on wife out for revenge?" Alice asked.

"No, Misty's not married," I said.

"I don't see the motive," Alice said. "She had nothing to gain from killing Connie, and plenty to lose."

I looked at the three expectant faces. "Which is why we need to find Misty and ask her if she had a reason for wanting Connie dead."

Chapter 19

I rubbed my eyes and poured strong coffee into a mug.

"Woof, woof." Meatball bounced around my feet. He ran to his empty bowl, returning and dropping it on my toes.

"Sorry, boy. I'm a bit slow today. Too little sleep and too much thinking." All night, I'd tried to figure out if Misty could be behind Connie's murder. I'd been so quick to dismiss her. She was friendly. She'd called herself a free spirit who loved animals. Misty was a good person.

And the biggest stumbling block was that we'd been together when Connie received her fatal dose of poison. How could she have murdered her? Had she planned it out so carefully? She killed Connie, then took Saffron for a walk and was able to act relaxed and happy? If I'd just murdered someone, I'd be a quivering, sweaty, adrenalin fueled wreck. I doubt I'd be able to get a sentence out straight. Yet Misty had been funny and charming when we'd met.

I poured kibble into Meatball's bowl and set it down for him.

He wagged his tail in appreciation, not seeming to hold a grudge that I moved at a snail's pace this morning.

I still wasn't convinced Misty was involved in Connie's murder, which was why I'd come up with a reason to speak with her today. It was the only thing I could think of that might make Misty angry. She loved animals, and Connie, well, at best, she'd been indifferent to Saffron. But was that enough of a reason for Misty to kill Connie?

I really wasn't sure, but I needed to move fast. The wedding fair was packing up this morning and some of the vendors had already left.

There was a knock on my apartment door. I downed my coffee, welcoming the caffeine hit, hurried over, and opened it.

Alice stood outside, an excited gleam in her eyes. "All set for our grand reveal?"

I scrubbed my eyes again. "Just about."

"Do you think Misty will believe your story?" Alice looked down at Meatball, who stood by my side, licking the last of his breakfast off his muzzle, his gaze on the lush green grass outside.

"I can put on an act. Make it convincing."

She tilted her head. "Everyone can see how much you love Meatball."

"Misty doesn't know me that well. And I needed a reason to talk to her. It should be easy to convince her I need to find him a new home." I petted his head. "Which of course, I don't. Don't take anything I'm about to say to heart. You're staying with me."

"Woof, woof!" He wagged his tail like he knew that truth was written across my heart, then dodged around Alice's legs to sniff the grass.

"I hope you don't mind, but we've got reinforcements," Alice said.

I grabbed my jacket, locked the door of the apartment, and headed outside. "What are you talking about?"

She clasped her hands together, a guilty look on her face. "I didn't mean to say anything, but I was so excited and it just slipped out."

Worry slid through me. "Alice, what did you do?"

"I saw Campbell. I asked him how things were going with Leanna. He said they're holding her for further questioning. The police think she's guilty."

"I understand why they're doing that," I said. "I thought she was guilty when I spotted her running away."

"But we know she's innocent."

"Probably innocent. I'm still not sold on Misty being the killer. But—"

"She could have slipped Connie poison, the same as Leanna. We have to be sure. And, so …" She looked away and twisted a strand of hair around her fingers.

"I know you haven't gotten to the worst bit. Spit it out, this is getting painful."

"When I was talking to Campbell, I mentioned your theory that Misty killed Connie."

I groaned. "I bet he was thrilled to learn I'm still investigating."

"Not exactly. He told me the case was almost solved and I don't need to worry. I told him I was worried. And … well, I insisted he search Misty's campervan."

I grabbed her arm and spun her toward me. "You did what? If she finds out, that'll give the game away. When Misty discovers Campbell at her door—"

"No! I told him what we were planning. I said we'd talk to Misty and figure out the motive for her wanting Connie dead. I then instructed him to look in the campervan when Misty is out with the dogs."

"He's going to kill me." I hid my face in my hands for a second. "He'll think I put you up to this."

Alice giggled. "Campbell did mention your name several times. But I didn't say a word. Besides, I fully support this idea. It's important to cover all the bases. Misty may have some poison hidden in her campervan. It could be the clue we need to show she's guilty."

"Or it could mean Campbell's about to put an enormous target on my back and take me down the next chance he gets."

"Stop panicking. We needed a backup plan," Alice said. "What if we can't get anything useful out of Misty? Then we'll be stumped. She'll vanish off into the sunset and Leanna could take the fall for what she did."

I tried to ignore the tingles down my spine telling me to pack a bag and leave the country before Campbell caught up with me. "It's not a bad idea to have a backup plan."

"I do have good ideas, occasionally," Alice said. "Campbell is waiting until Misty leaves to walk the dogs. Then he's doing a search. The police are on standby and a warrant's been issued, so if any evidence is found, it'll hold up in court."

I stared at her. "You're getting really good at this. Maybe I should retire from being the nosy one in this partnership."

"Don't you dare! And I've learned everything from you. Oh, and the back-to-back episodes of those crime scene investigation programs I've been watching. They're so useful, if a little bloody. And some of the male actors are delicious."

"If this doesn't work out, Campbell will never speak to me again. He may not speak to you, either."

"He has to speak to me. I'm his boss, technically. And he'll get over it. He'll have a grumpy couple of days, then be back to normal once he realizes how brilliant we are. That's just how he is."

"Let's hope so. Come on. We need to get a move on if we're going to find Misty out with the dogs."

She skipped along beside me. "Hopefully, we can solve this quickly and have a celebratory breakfast. You can make waffles."

"I'd be honored to serve you, milady." I tugged on an imaginary cap.

She thumped me in the arm. "I prefer your highness."

I laughed, still tense despite Alice's reassurances. Campbell would be so angry with me, but if we solved this crime, he'd just have to get over himself.

We headed toward the trees where I'd seen Misty walking the dogs on several occasions.

It didn't take long before Meatball raced off, his ears pricked as he detected other dogs up ahead.

There was a round of sharp barking, and I heard Misty's voice in the distance.

"There's our target," I said.

"I'll stay quiet. You do the talking," Alice said.

We increased our pace and discovered Misty in a clearing with Saffron.

She raised a hand when she saw me and Alice. "I figured you must be somewhere nearby if this little guy was racing around."

"Hi. Just having our morning walk." I strolled over, trying to look calm, unlike my hammering heart. "How are you doing with the new addition to your family?"

"I'm still struggling a bit with Saffron." She had the little dog in her arms. Saffron was growling and baring her teeth at Meatball, who looked up at her and wagged his tail.

"It'll take a while to train the bad habits out of her," I said.

"We'll get there. She's a beautiful work in progress," Misty said.

"Did you hear about what happened to Leanna?" I asked. "She's been taken in for questioning about Connie's murder."

Misty focused on Saffron and straightened her collar. "I did. I was surprised. I figured if anyone killed Connie it would have been Belinda. Shows what I know."

"Belinda had an alibi," I said. "Leanna didn't. It looks like she'll be charged with murder."

Misty shook her head. "It's a real shame. But Connie could be a tough woman. And she had no maternal instinct, no ability to nurture or support. She never had children of her own."

"She had Saffron," I said. "Maybe Connie preferred fur babies to real babies."

Misty still didn't meet my gaze as she snuggled Saffron to her chest. "She didn't treat Saffron like a baby. She didn't adore her like I do. She got her the same way people pick out a necklace. More of an accessory than a beloved member of the family. She carried Saffron around dressed in those ridiculous outfits and showed her off, posting pictures online for people to like and comment on. Dogs aren't like pieces of jewelry you can hang around your neck to impress others."

I nodded. Misty had the same views about animals as I did. Which didn't make what I was about to do any easier. "I'm glad I've caught you, actually. I need your advice. I'm thinking about giving up Meatball."

Misty's head shot up, and she stared at me. "Why would you do that? You're the perfect pair."

"Meatball gets a bit stinky when he eats too much," Alice said. "He lets off terrible smells. I can understand why Holly is having second thoughts about keeping him."

Meatball cocked his head at her.

I shrugged and tried to look nonchalant and unbothered that I was discussing giving up my furry best buddy. "That's true. I'm too busy to sort out a special diet for him.

And all the walking and clearing up gets boring. Plus, the vet's bills are so expensive."

Misty's mouth opened and closed several times. "You can't do that. Look at him, he loves you. He'd be heartbroken if you got rid of him."

As if I'd trained him to do it, Meatball bounced off his front paws and waggled them in the air at me, looking like the cutest, most adorable, pup in the world.

I ignored him, even though I wanted to drop to my knees and give him a huge belly rub. "You know that dogs can be a lot of work. They're almost as bad as having a baby." I glanced at Meatball and forced myself to frown. "He's cute, but I need to focus on my career. He gets in the way."

Misty pursed her lips, her eyes narrowing. "You sound like Connie. She thought having a puppy would be fun and get her lots of attention. She didn't think about all the work that went into raising a little one. As soon as she got bored with Saffron, she tossed her to one side like a worn sweater."

"And hired you to take care of her?" I said.

"I'd have done it for free if I could," Misty said. "That's no way to treat a dog. Of course, they need training, grooming, feeding, and walking. She mistreated this little one. That was wrong."

I glanced at Alice. We'd just found a motive. "Much like Alice and me, I expect it makes you sick when someone mistreats an animal."

"Of course! What kind of monster would hurt an animal?"

"Someone I'm happy not to be around. Was that why you poisoned Connie?" I asked.

Alice gave a little hiccupping gasp.

Misty's gaze moved slowly from me to Alice and back again. "Why do you think I poisoned her?"

"Connie was mistreating Saffron. You couldn't bear to see that, so you did something about it," I said.

Misty shook her head. "Leanna did it. The police wouldn't have taken her away if they didn't think she was guilty."

"Leanna was planning her future. She wasn't staying with Connie much longer. Why kill her when she already had an exit plan?" I asked.

Misty shrugged. "I've no idea. Maybe Connie did something so bad that she couldn't take it any longer. She had a cruel side to her."

"Or maybe Leanna didn't poison her." I took a step closer. "You told me you were friends with Connie. Why would you be friends with someone who mistreated their animal?"

She sighed. "Okay, I'm not sad Connie is dead. It served her right. She was horrible to everyone. She was really mean to Leanna, and treated me like a slave, sometimes. If it wasn't for the fact I loved this little dog, I'd have handed in my notice and left her in the lurch ages ago. She knew how much I cared for Saffron and exploited that."

"Connie doesn't sound like a great person, but she shouldn't have been poisoned. What did you use?" I asked.

"Nothing! This has nothing to do with me. Holly, I considered you a friend. Well, I did until you asked about getting rid of your dog. I had you all wrong. I thought we understood each other."

"Campbell's coming," Alice whispered in my ear. She turned and hurried over to him.

Misty took a step back, her hands tightening around Saffron. "What's going on? What did you do?"

"Misty, I understand if you wanted Connie dead. Animal cruelty is wrong, and it makes me so angry. Any animal just wants to be loved and looked after. They put their faith and trust in us, but sometimes it goes wrong."

"It definitely went wrong with Connie. That woman had no heart. All she cared about was how much money she could make. It was disgusting."

"And you did something about it. When did it first start?"

She shook her head again. "I'm saying nothing."

Campbell strode over with Alice by his side, his expression dark.

"Did you find anything?" I asked him.

"What are you talking about?" Misty's wide-eyed gaze shot to Campbell.

"We did. The search warrants got us what we needed," Campbell said.

"Hold on! You've been searching my things while I've been away from my campervan. That's illegal. You had no right."

"We had every right," Campbell said.

Misty huffed out a breath. "I look after the animals in that van. I'd never risk their safety by having anything poisonous around. I even keep the cleaning products locked in a cupboard so they can't get to them."

"You're right. We found nothing in your campervan," Campbell said.

Misty jabbed a finger at me. "You see. I had nothing to do with what happened to Connie."

"However, we did find several bottles of antifreeze in your apartment," Campbell said.

Alice gave a squeak of delight and bounced on her toes.

"You searched Misty's apartment?" I asked.

"I didn't, but the police in her local area did when I got in touch and explained the situation. We arranged for a search warrant on the apartment and the campervan so nothing was missed," Campbell said.

"That proves nothing." Misty shifted Saffron in her arms. "I expect most people have antifreeze in their home or garage. It's useful when it gets cold."

"How did you give Connie the antifreeze? In her tea?" I asked. "I saw a picture of you handing her a mug."

Misty looked away, her fingers flexing around Saffron. "I can't answer that, because I didn't do it."

"That method wouldn't be reliable," Campbell said. "If Connie only drank a small amount of the poisoned liquid, it wouldn't have affected her."

"So, you put it in her food?" I asked Misty.

"No, you'd have the same problem," Campbell said. "You only need about a third of a cup of antifreeze to kill someone."

"And you couldn't guarantee the antifreeze would be evenly distributed if you baked it in a cake. Connie might not have gotten any poison. Unless ..." I tapped my finger against my chin. "If Misty gave Connie individual cupcakes or muffins—"

"Like the ones you serve in the café," Alice said.

I nodded. "That would be a safe way to make sure Connie got the right dose. The antifreeze could be added after each cake had been baked. Just enough to make Connie sick. You told me you often had tea and cake with her," I said to Misty. "Is that how you did it? You added the poison to the cake, making sure she got the dosed piece?"

Misty swallowed audibly. "So, I liked to bake for Connie. That's no crime."

A shudder ran through me. "Lady Diana ate that brownie Connie gave her the day we looked around the wedding fair. Then she got sick."

Alice's eyes widened, and she looked back at the castle. "I thought she'd contracted the stomach bug other people have been suffering with. You don't think—"

"No!" Misty's bottom lip wobbled. "No one else was supposed to get hurt."

Alice's eyes filled with tears. "Campbell, help! Diana's been poisoned. She's going to die just like Connie."

"Misty, did you put antifreeze in Connie's brownie? Is Lady Diana at risk?" I grabbed her arm.

She looked down at Saffron and softly stroked her head. "I did. Connie didn't deserve to live, but I only meant for her to receive the poison. She shouldn't have given her food away."

Campbell took a step back, already speaking to someone using his comms device.

My gaze went to Saffron who was snuggled against Misty's chest, her eyes half closed. "You did it to protect the dog. You thought she was mistreating Saffron."

"I didn't think, I saw it with my own eyes. Connie was abusing her. It wasn't that she just used her as an accessory, dressing her up in outfits and shoving her in those oversized purses she carried around, she hit her. Saffron was so terrified that she used to wet on the floor, and that made Connie angrier. I had to stop the abuse."

"You could have suggested she treat her animal better," Campbell said as he re-joined the group.

Alice grabbed his arm. "What's happening to Diana? She's been a proper grump recently, but I don't want to lose her. She's my third favorite cousin."

"I have a man with her now. And an ambulance has been called." Campbell briefly held Alice's hand. "She should be fine."

"She'll be okay. One dose won't kill her," Misty said. "And there won't be any lasting damage so long as she gets treated."

Alice tugged on Campbell's arm. "Is that true?"

"Most likely. It takes a large dose to cause organ failure."

"And Misty would know all about that, because she's been using it on Connie for months," I said.

Misty ducked her head. "I wasn't sure how much to use, so I started small. A few drops to begin with. I promise you, I tried everything to get her to change how she treated Saffron. She had every chance to be a better dog mother. I suggested positive reinforcement, treats, and kind words. Connie dismissed the ideas. She said her parents used physical punishment on her when she was a child and she'd grown up just fine." She snorted, her expression tight. "Everyone could see that wasn't true. Connie was sharp with everyone. I don't think she knew how to love. She used men and tossed them aside, she was unkind to anyone who worked with her, me included, but worst of all, she hurt this innocent baby." She kissed the top of Saffron's head.

I felt a degree of sympathy for Misty. "Why didn't you have Saffron removed from her care?"

"She'd have just gotten another dog and treated it as badly. I even said I'd take Saffron and look after her, but Connie wouldn't hear of it. She claimed to like having her around, but she barely paid Saffron any attention, and when she did, it was only to yell at her. She should have been banned from having animals."

"What pushed you over the edge?" I asked. "You were trying to make her change, but something happened that made you finally kill her."

Misty glanced up at me, her eyes full of regret. "Connie started talking about getting more dogs. I tried to dissuade her, but she was already in contact with several breeders, looking for a puppy. The poor thing would have had a hideous life alongside Saffron. She told me two weeks ago that she was meeting a breeder to look at some pups and wanted me to go with her after the wedding fair."

"And you couldn't bear seeing another animal suffer," I said.

"That doesn't make it right," Campbell muttered.

That was true, but it made it more understandable. "Why use this particular poison?" I asked.

"I wanted Connie to feel pain, fear, and out of control, just like she'd made Saffron feel." Misty lifted her chin. "Although it only made her temper worse when she wasn't feeling well. She lashed out at everyone."

"So Saffron suffered even more," I said.

Misty's lips thinned. "Connie always wore those awful pointed toed high heels. Saffron got in her way and she kicked her. The poor dog yelped and ran away. That was it. I couldn't take anymore. What with the abuse and the looming prospect of another puppy, I had to act. I didn't plan on killing Connie to begin with, I just wanted to make her suffer. I hoped she'd understand how miserable it was to feel scared and have no one look after you. I got it wrong. She turned into an even worse monster."

"You put the final fatal dose in her food?" I asked. "It was enough to kill her swiftly, but it gave you enough time to get away so you were nowhere near her body when she was found."

"Yes, it was easy to do. Connie used to tease me that I was a hippie because I loved using wild plants and herbs in my food. I collected them when out dog walking. She was always dieting, and rarely ate chocolate, but had a real sweet tooth. Connie would happily eat the muffins or brownies I made. I'd tell her they were all natural ingredients and not fattening. And antifreeze has a sweet taste, so she suspected nothing. I quadrupled the dose the day she died. I put it in her tea and cake to make sure she wouldn't survive."

"Then left her to die," I said.

"I'm not sorry it happened. The world is a better place without her in it," Misty said.

"Let's continue this conversation at the police station." Campbell walked over to Misty and caught hold of her arm.

"What about the dogs I'm looking after?" Misty said. "I can't leave them. And Saffron has no one. I'm not letting her go to the pound. She'll be terrified."

"Leave her with me." I held out my hands. "She'll be safe."

"How do I know that? You were just talking about giving up your own dog and what a hassle he was. And that ..." Her eyes widened. "Oh! You tricked me."

I lowered my hands. "I had to figure out what your motive was for wanting Connie dead. As soon as I saw your reaction when I said I wanted to give up Meatball, it clicked into place. You'd do anything to protect the dogs you love. I understand. And I'd never let go of Meatball. He's my best friend."

Misty's shoulders slumped. She cuddled Saffron for a few more seconds before placing another kiss on her head. "You go with this nice lady. She'll look after you." She handed her to me.

Saffron grumbled for a few seconds. She finally settled in my arms, blinking her big eyes up at me.

"I'll make sure no one ever hurts you again," I said to Saffron. "I promise you that."

"Let's move," Campbell said.

"Holly, let the other dog owners know I won't be available today," Misty said. "I hate to let them down."

"Of course. Don't worry about the dogs."

Her gaze was on Saffron. "That's all I do. Dogs are my life. And as you've just discovered, I'd kill to protect them."

I stood with Alice and Meatball as Campbell led Misty away.

Alice went to stroke Saffron, but she growled at her. "Hmmm, I'm not sure I'd kill to save this little one. She's a bit grumpy."

"You'd be grumpy too if you'd been abused by your owner." I tickled Saffron under the chin. "I don't suppose you want to take her on?"

Alice's nose wrinkled. "No, she's not the dog for me. She reminds me too much of Diana. And having to put up with a sick, grumpy cousin is more than enough. I don't need a grumpy dog, too."

"Aren't you worried about Lady Diana being poisoned?"

"A little, but Campbell is on top of things. And Misty said Diana won't die from a single dose of antifreeze." Alice groaned. "I bet she'll be even more sullen when she finds out she was poisoned. She'll blame it on me."

I smirked and shook my head. "It's reassuring to see you so concerned for your family's welfare."

"I am! I mean, I would be more concerned if she was a bit nicer to me. She can be so horrible."

"Alice!"

"Oh, fine. I'll send her some flowers and listen to her whine about surviving death and blah blah blah."

"You should let Percy know what happened."

She nudged me. "That's a genius idea. He might realize how much he still loves her and take her off my hands."

"You're all heart."

"I am with the people I really love." She nudged me again with her hip. "What will you do with Saffron?"

"I'm sure she someone's perfect little dog. I just need to find that someone she fits with."

"Maybe she could settle in with you and Meatball."

Meatball whined and lowered his ears.

I grinned. "Don't worry, I don't think you and Saffron will ever be friends. I won't force you to share your bed with her."

"Killing for a dog," Alice said as we walked slowly back to the castle. "I admire Misty's spirit. She's a protector of the weak."

"She's also a killer. Come on, let's get back to the wedding fair and speak to the other dog owners so they know Misty's out of action. Then you need to go and see Lady Diana, while I figure out what to do with Saffron."

Chapter 20

"Gran, have you seen Saffron?" I headed into the lounge, a smile crossing my face as I discovered the dog snuggled on her lap.

It had been three days since Misty's arrest, and life was almost back to normal.

Gran grinned up at me. "I've never been into small dogs, but this one is growing on me."

I sat next to her and stroked Saffron's head. "She's a little cutie. Although she still doesn't get along with Meatball."

Meatball sat on the other side of the lounge in his fluffy dog bed, an unhappy look on his face and possibly a hint of jealousy shining in his eyes as he watched us.

"I'm sure he'll win her round given enough time," Gran said. She patted my hand. "I'm so impressed with your detective skills. You solved a murder."

"You know me, I love to solve puzzles. I blame you for that."

"I'll happily take the blame if it means you put dangerous people away," Gran said. "How much does it pay?"

"Pay! Gran, I don't do it for the money. I do it so criminals get what they deserve."

She was silent for a moment, her fingers running over Saffron's fur. "What do you think I deserve?"

"What do you mean?"

"Well, I stole Tina's purse, set up a fake raffle, and took Leanna's laptop. Doesn't that also make me a criminal?"

I let out a soft sigh. It was a gray area. If I did want to see criminals get what they deserved, I should turn Gran over to the police and tell them everything.

"There are mitigating circumstances when it comes to your crimes," I finally said.

A slow smile spread across her face. "And what would they be?"

"You helped to solve this murder. I may not have figured out who Tina was if you hadn't lifted her purse, and I certainly wouldn't have connected the poisonings to Misty if I hadn't seen the pictures Leanna had on her laptop. You helped provide the clues that solved this case."

She sat up straight and gave a nod. "Too right I did. I should get a full pardon and a clean slate for my contribution to justice. A salary and a place to live would also be good."

I chuckled. "Maybe we won't go that far."

"And let's not forget, the local animal shelter also got a nice donation thanks to my generous raffle donors. I'm practically a saint." Gran sank back in her seat, one hand on Saffron. "I'm glad I could help you, Holly. Even in a small way."

"So am I. It's great having you here," I said.

A knock at the door interrupted us.

"That's most likely Alice." I bit my bottom lip. "I'm almost scared to open the door. She's organized the fancy dress outfits for the plogging event."

"I can't wait to see you all running around the village dressed as fairies or whatever she has planned for you."

"I should force you to take part," I said.

"Maybe I will. Although I have no costume. I guess I'll sit this one out."

I hurried to the door and opened it. I took a step back, a startled laugh shooting out of me. "You look …"

"You can say it. I look incredible." Alice turned slowly. She wore an enormous T-Rex costume in a gray and mottled green. It came with a wobbly head, tiny arms, and a huge tail.

Rupert stood next to her, dressed in exactly the same costume. He gave me a sheepish grin. "This was all my sister's idea."

"I … wow! I figured you'd come as some kind of fairy princess. Why dinosaurs?" I stepped back to allow them inside.

Alice squeezed through the front door, her huge tail almost sweeping a side table over. "I want us to stand out. And I need our team to look fearsome. What's better than a terrifying dinosaur that could eat a human in a single bite?"

"Wait, you said team. You've got me a T-Rex costume, too?"

"Of course. Rupert, bring it in." Alice gestured at him.

Meatball hopped up from his bed. He sniffed around Alice's costume with a great deal of interest before giving the tail a tentative bite.

"You keep your paws off my tail." Alice scooped it out of his reach. "I'm an apex predator, and you look like a tasty snack." She waggled her T-Rex head at him.

Meatball wagged his tail, then turned to me, his look suggesting he was bewildered by Alice's transformation.

"What do we have here?" Gran wandered out of the lounge with Saffron in her arms.

"Hi, Holly's gran," Alice said. "Are you taking part in the plogging event?"

"I will if I get my own dinosaur costume."

I turned and stared at her. "Gran! Really?"

"Of course. It'll be a fun thing to do on my first date with Ray."

My mouth dropped open. "You've got a date?"

She gave me a sly smile. "We got talking after he helped us investigate the different poisons. He's such a clever man and very handsome. I asked him if he was going to the event and he said he wasn't sure. I convinced him he should come with me."

"That's even better." Alice clapped her small dinosaur hands together. "The more the merrier on our team, especially since we're up against the pterodactyls."

"This isn't a competitive event." I stepped out of the way as Rupert came in with an enormous costume for me.

"It absolutely is," Alice said. "Rupert, get one of the spare costumes I ordered. Holly's gran is taking part as well. Yay! T-Rex for the win."

He sighed before shuffling out the door, muttering under his breath about being his mean sister's slave.

"Exactly who are the pterodactyls?" I asked.

"Campbell and his security team, of course," Alice said. "I ordered them all costumes. I told him what he'd be wearing yesterday."

I pressed my hand against my forehead, not sure whether to laugh or retreat to my bed. "I bet he loved that idea."

"He took some persuading, but I said it was for a good cause and would be great publicity for the castle. I also said I was attending with Rupert, so he'd have to be there and blend in. I did have to get a bit stern with him when he said he wasn't sure he'd fit in a costume. Although they do come up on the small side."

I chuckled. "I have to see his costume. Let me get changed and then we can go. Gran, are you sure you want in?"

"Absolutely. Give me my costume. I'll go get changed and call Ray before we leave, to see what team he's on. Princess Alice, can you only be a T-Rex or a pterodactyl?"

"No, Ray can come as anything he likes," Alice said. "So long as he dresses up."

Gran took the costume from Rupert and headed into the lounge.

I was already dressed in my running gear, so it wasn't tricky to slip into the dinosaur costume and shimmy the tail and head into place.

"You look amazing," Alice said. "Almost as good as me. I'm queen dino, though."

"They had dinosaur queens in the Cretaceous period?" I asked.

"It's debatable. After all, they died out, so it was most likely the boys in charge, messing around and being idiots," Alice said.

"We aren't all idiots," Rupert said.

"You definitely are. You put your costume on the wrong way round when you got it," Alice said.

"Anyone could make that mistake. The holes are confusing." Rupert stubbed his huge clawed foot on the floor.

I hadn't spoken to him since the awkward incident in the rose garden. I hated that there was distance between us. "Rupert, I got you something."

His head shot up. "You have?"

"I went to Artfully Homewares yesterday and collected our pots. Do you want to take a look at the finished result?"

His bright smile lifted my mood. "Of course. I'd forgotten about those."

"You went to Artfully Homewares without me?" Alice lifted her dinosaur head and scowled at me. "Why wasn't I invited?"

"It was a last-minute thing." I shared a grin with Rupert. "We bumped into each other and decided to give it a go."

"Hmmm. Well, next time, ask me along. I'll have a driver bring me," she said.

"Definitely next time. Wait right here." I shuffled away in my T-Rex costume and returned with the pots, no easy feat now I had tiny arms and rather pathetic grasping claws. I'd painted mine with miniature cherry topped muffins. Rupert had gone for a book theme, given his love of poetry.

He took his pot and turned it over several times. "They look great. Thanks for picking them up."

"You're welcome."

His gaze went to my pot. "Perhaps we could swap."

"Sure. Take a look at mine. A couple of the muffins are wonky, though."

He took it, his cheeks burning and his gaze glued to the pot. "I meant for good. I keep your pot and you can have mine. It'll be a nice reminder of our ... time together."

"Oh! Well ..." I looked at Alice. She was grinning and inspecting her claws. "Sure. I'd like that."

He handed me his pot and dazzled me with another smile. "I shall put it in pride of place in my room."

I suddenly felt very warm in my costume. I set his pot down and adjusted my giant head. "This tail will slow me down when I'm plogging."

"You can sweep up loads of trash with that tail," Alice said. "It's an asset."

Meatball trotted over, cocked his head, and stared at me in disbelief.

"Don't think you're getting out of this." Alice produced a soft mottled green play suit from inside her costume and held it out to him.

"I, um, Meatball's not that crazy about wearing outfits." I eyed the outfit as suspiciously as he did.

"I know that! It clips to his collar and sits on his back. No stuffing his little legs into anything in an undignified way. He'll look adorable. And if he really hates it, I'll take it off." Alice awkwardly kneeled in front of Meatball. Her T-Rex head almost swallowed him as she bent forward and attached the dinosaur outfit.

He shook a few times and sniffed at it, but then wagged his tail.

"He loves it!" Alice hopped in the air, making the costume jiggle like a moldy green jelly. "He has to be on our team."

"What do you think?" Gran appeared, dressed as a T-Rex. Saffron was trotting at her heel, glancing at Gran and occasionally growling.

"It's a unique outfit for a first date," Alice said. "Now, we need to get a move on. We don't want to be late."

We squeezed out the front door, the dogs coming with us.

"I'm so glad this horrible business at the wedding fair is resolved," Alice said. "Everyone's gone now. Things are back to normal, and we have the grounds to ourselves, completely free of trouble makers, poisoners, and snooty wedding planners."

I nodded, concentrating on walking in my new giant feet.

"The other suspects must have been shocked to learn it was Misty," Gran said.

"I was. I never imagined it was her. Holly figured that one out," Alice said. She looked down at Saffron, who trotted along beside Gran, a besotted expression on her face. "What will happen to Connie's dog?"

"I've come to a decision about that," Gran said. "I'm keeping her. It'll do me good to have someone to look after. Make me more responsible." She looked at me and winked.

"That's the perfect solution," Alice said. "Saffron has taken to you."

"It's a great idea," I said. "Are you sure you can manage her?"

"I've got a few things to sort out," Gran said, "but it'll be fine. I need to find a place to live that'll accept dogs, but she's so tiny, people won't even notice her if I have to sneak her in."

I grinned and squeezed her elbow through the costume. Saffron was just what Gran needed, some stability in her life and a bit of responsibility. And Saffron would be spoiled rotten by Gran. We were both big animal lovers. She would never have to feel scared again now she had her new home.

"It'll take too long to walk to the village dressed like this, so I've got a car waiting for us," Alice said.

I was so relieved to hear that, I could have hugged her. We bundled into the large SUV, tails flapping and heads bobbing.

As we pulled up at the central meeting spot for the start of the plogging event, I was delighted to see a huge group of people. And it looked like everyone had gotten the fancy dress message. There was an array of outfits, including a giraffe, a pirate, and a witch. I focused on the large group of imposing pterodactyls staked out in one corner.

"I still can't believe you convinced Campbell and his team to dress up," I said to Alice as we forced our way out of the car.

Alice's eyes widened as she stared at Campbell. "Oh, my! I didn't expect the outfits to be quite so ... figure hugging. You can see everything." Her cheeks flushed pink.

Campbell and his team had large wobbly pterodactyl hats on their heads and wings strapped to their backs. They all wore mottled brown cat suits. And Alice was right, they left nothing to the imagination. There were muscles bulging and all sorts of interesting lumps and bumps on display.

"You need to stop drooling," I whispered to her.

She snapped her jaw shut. "I wasn't. But I mean, look at him. In fact, all of his team look incredible. I should suggest the security team wear something like that all the time."

I laughed out loud. "Alice! Don't you dare. Although it would be hilarious to watch Campbell walking around dressed like that and trying to be all cool and mysterious."

"I'll give it some thought," Alice said.

"You do that. I need to get to work." I spent the next half an hour checking everyone was happy, answering any questions, and handing out recycling bags for people to collect their trash in. A hundred people had shown up, which I was thrilled about. And I was amazed to see Lady Diana there, although she wasn't in a costume.

"It's good to see you up and about," I said to her.

She looked away, her chin pointed up. "I'm still feeling sick. I can't believe that witch poisoned me."

"By accident. Misty was trying to kill someone else."

"That doesn't make me feel any better." Lady Diana rubbed her stomach.

"Is someone coming to take you home?"

"Yes. I wanted to wait at the castle, but Alice insisted I come to this event. So, I'm here, but I never said I'd take part. Anyway, my husband is coming for me."

"That's great news. You're back together?"

She turned to me, her eyes cold. "You may feel free to speak about any subject with my ridiculous cousins, but we aren't friends. Keep your questions and opinions to yourself."

I backed away and held my hands up. I did sometimes forget my place. "My apologies."

"Is there a problem?" Alice strode over.

Lady Diana glanced her way and scowled. "Your ... friend was being impertinent."

"Sorry, Lady Diana, it won't happen again." I turned to go.

"No! You wait right here." Alice grabbed my claw. "Holly is my friend. A really good one. The best friend I've ever had. Show her some respect."

Lady Diana turned away. "Why should I? She was being nosy."

"I expect Holly was actually being kind to you. A concept you don't understand," Alice said.

Lady Diana's mouth dropped open as she turned back to us. "You're siding with her? But we're family."

Alice huffed out a breath. "Holly is like a sister to me. You can't be mean to her."

"Alice, it's okay. I should get on." I didn't want to cause a family feud, and I had over-stepped the mark by asking about Lady Diana's marriage.

"It's not okay. You were the one who figured out Diana had been poisoned. If it weren't for you, she could have permanent kidney damage." Alice jabbed a claw at her. "She should be thanking you."

"There's no need," I said.

"Did you?" Lady Diana turned her full attention on me. "You discovered I'd been poisoned with antifreeze?"

"Yes." I drew the word out slowly.

She sniffed. "Well, I suppose I should show some gratitude and thank you."

"Do it, then," Alice said.

Lady Diana walked away. "I just did. And there's my husband's driver. I'm leaving."

We stood side by side and watched her go.

"If she wasn't my cousin, I'd never speak to her again," Alice said.

I hugged her as best I could in my costume. "Thanks for coming to my rescue. I put my foot right in it."

"Any time. That's what queen dinosaurs do for their dinosaur minions. I couldn't let her bite your head off."

I laughed and headed over to Campbell's team. I couldn't help but grin when I stopped in front of him. "You all look amazing. Top marks for effort."

Campbell glowered at me. "We look ridiculous. But Princess Alice left me with no choice."

"Did she threaten to put your team in the dungeon if you didn't dress as pterodactyls?"

He arched an eyebrow. "You know her too well. She talked at me for at least an hour, coming up with different reasons why we had to dress like this." He raised a brown wing and snorted. "How am I supposed to pick up trash with this thing hanging off my arm?"

"If you want a real challenge, you should try picking up trash with tiny dinosaur claws that don't close properly." I waggled a wobbly hand at him.

"It seems she has us both at a disadvantage."

"This event is more about fun and bringing the village together," I said. "And as long as we get round to picking up all the trash, that's the main thing."

"I still plan on beating you," he said. "Regardless of the stupid pterodactyl wings."

"Is that so? Well, I plan on beating you, even though I have ridiculously small arms that don't pick anything up."

He smirked before walking us away from his team so they couldn't overhear us. "Good call on the Misty business."

"You're very welcome. Any time you need my help in the future, you only have to ask."

"Don't get smug. It's not attractive."

"Says the person who walks around looking permanently smug."

"I have a right to look smug. I'm the best at what I do."

I snorted a laugh. "How's everything going with Misty?"

"She's talking, and she hasn't changed her story. Although she does keep asking about Saffron."

"You can tell her she's safe. I've been looking after her these past few days, and my gran's decided to take her on. She's great with animals. We had dogs when I was growing up, so she knows how to look after her."

"Good to know. I'll pass on the information. It's irritating being asked the same thing over and over again. Sometimes, people just don't know when to keep quiet."

I sidestepped the insult. "I sympathize with Misty. She had a good reason for stopping Connie."

"You're justifying her actions?"

"I'm just saying, that I'd kill anyone if they hurt Meatball."

"I'll bear that in mind, Holmes."

"You do that. I look after my own. Meatball is like family to me."

"About that." He turned his head and his pterodactyl hat whacked the nose of my T-Rex. "Your gran's background makes for interesting reading."

I swallowed and glanced over at Gran. "You've been checking her out?"

"She's been spending time around the family, of course I'm going to check her out. Why didn't you tell me who she was and where she's been?"

"Because I knew you'd get that look on your face that suggests you want to get rid of her. She's no trouble."

"Of course she's trouble. You're as bad as each other. Do you want to tell me what she's been up to while she's been here? There have been several reports of purses going missing."

"There's nothing to tell." I ducked my head, grateful the dinosaur outfit hid my expression.

"You want to answer that again?"

"Not really."

He crossed his arms over his chest, bending the wings around him. It was impressively intimidating. He looked like a stone age Batman.

"Gran is … adjusting." I met his gaze. "She's not perfect, but she's doing her best. And I think it's great she's got Saffron to take care of. It'll give her something positive to focus on."

"So, she's not a reformed character? She could turn to crime again?"

"She'll do her best not to. Plus, she's got Saffron now, and she's going on a date with Ray today. Those are both good things. That's all she needs, some positivity in her life. And before you freak out about her past, she had her reasons for doing what she did."

"I know what her reasons were," Campbell said. "I don't agree with them. If she causes any trouble while she's here, I'm coming for you. You're the reason she's staying in the village. Don't think she gets a free pass because she's your gran."

"I'd never imagine you'd do that," I said. "You're always on the right side of the law."

"And you sometimes aren't, which is where we clash."

"Not deliberately. And it gets the job done. Connie's killer was brought to justice."

"You got lucky with her."

I bumped him with my T-Rex head. "You can think what you like. I helped you. One day, you'll stop resenting that."

"It won't be any time soon. Now, how about you get this plogging event going so I can whip your behind."

"My T-Rex will eat you alive."

He whacked the top of my dinosaur head with a wing. "Challenge accepted."

I headed back to Alice and Rupert. Gran was standing a short distance away, Saffron in her arms as she chatted to Ray. Meatball was bounding around checking out all the costumes.

"I think everyone's ready to go." I looked at Alice and Rupert. "Shall we get started?"

They nodded.

"Let's beat those pterodactyls," Alice said.

I turned and faced the crowd. "Everybody, I'd like to welcome you to the first ever plogging event in Audley St. Mary. This is our chance to give a little back to our beautiful village by making sure it's free from trash. I hope everyone has a bag to collect their trash."

People waved their bags at me.

"Excellent. Once your bag gets full, come find me, and I'll give you another one."

"And just to add a little excitement to this event," Alice said as she stepped forward, "the individual who fills the most sacks full of trash gets a gift card for Harrods and free afternoon tea at the castle café."

An excited murmur ran through the group.

"That's generous of you," I whispered to her.

She shrugged. "Why not? We'll incentivize everyone into being extra speedy."

"Is everybody ready to plog?" I asked.

A cheer went up.

"In three, two, one. Let's get plogging."

Campbell and his team took off, their wings wobbling as they raced around grabbing the trash as he barked instructions, coordinating them like they were on a military operation.

I headed off in the opposite direction with Alice and Rupert, our tails whacking on the ground. Meatball raced along beside me, grabbing at my tail, thinking this was one big game.

I waved at Gran as I jogged past her. "Having fun?"

She grinned and bobbed her T-Rex head. "Best date ever, so far."

Ray nodded and smiled at me.

As I jogged along, Campbell flashed me a wicked smile, the challenge clear in his eyes.

I couldn't help but laugh. Some things never changed in Audley St. Mary. And I was glad of it.

About Author

K.E. O'Connor (Karen) is a cozy mystery author living in the beautiful British countryside. She loves all things mystery, animals, and cake (these often feature in her books.)

When she's not writing about mysteries, murder, and treats, she volunteers at a local animal sanctuary, reads a ton of books, binge watches mystery series on TV, and dreams about living somewhere warmer.

To stay in touch with the fun, clean mysteries, where the killer always gets their just desserts:

Newsletter: www.subscribepage.com/cozymysteries
Website: www.keoconnor.com/writing
Facebook: www.facebook.com/keoconnorauthor

Also By

Enjoy the complete Holly Holmes cozy culinary mysteries in paperback or e-book.

Cream Caramel and Murder
Chocolate Swirls and Murder
Vanilla Whip and Murder
Cherry Cream and Murder
Blueberry Blast and Murder
Mocha Cream and Murder
Lemon Drizzle and Murder
Maple Glaze and Murder
Mint Frosting and Murder

Read on for a peek at book six in the series - Mocha Cream and Murder!

Chapter 1

"You should come with me to take a look." Granny Molly pushed her plate away and patted her stomach. "I'd like your opinion on the place."

"You don't have to move out of here if you don't want to. There's no hurry." I stood to take our empty plates from the table, but Gran waved at me to stay sitting.

"I'll wash up. After all, you cooked such a delicious meal. I've never tasted such incredible roast potatoes."

"You mean, I did an amazing job of reheating leftovers I snuck out of the kitchen because it was only going to be thrown away." That was one of the many benefits of working at Audley Castle. You were always guaranteed delicious food.

Gran grabbed the empty plates and carried them to the sink, her newly acquired dog, Saffron, glued to her heel. "Holly, I want to do my bit while I'm living under your roof."

"I really don't mind you staying longer." I'd enjoyed having Gran back. She'd been out of my life for too long.

"As sweet as your apartment is, you only have one bedroom. And I can't keep getting under your feet. Plus, Meatball is having to put up with this little madam's sass."

She looked down at Saffron. "Besides, it's not as if you invited me to stay." She turned and smiled, her warm, open face taking me back to the fun we had together when I was growing up.

"I feel like I've only just got you back, and you're leaving already."

"We'll have none of that nonsense. And I didn't exactly have a choice but to leave you. I had the offer of a comfortable single bed in a delightful prison cell. I could hardly turn that down."

I shook my head. As much as I loved Gran, I didn't love her inability to avoid getting involved in dodgy deals. It was something she was working on.

"I'm happy to come look at the place with you. It's on the corner of the village green, isn't it?" I said.

"Yes. I'll have a great view of all the comings and goings of the locals. I could even make some new friends."

"You already have a new friend. Ray. I thought maybe you'd take him along to have a look, since you're getting along well."

A faint blush rose on her cheeks. Gran was an attractive older lady with a good figure. It was no surprise she still had guys chasing after her.

She turned away and ran water into the sink. "We are getting along well, but we don't need to rush things."

"Maybe you should. You're not getting any younger."

She flicked soap suds at me. "Less of your cheek. There's plenty of life left in these bones."

A knock at the front door of my apartment had us turning.

Gran checked the time on the wall clock. "It's getting late. Are you expecting a visitor?"

I shook my head as I walked to the door. Meatball, my adorable corgi-cross, was right by my heels. Saffron was close behind, always keen to see what was going on.

"No. Let's see who it is." I pulled open the door.

Chef Heston stood there looking flushed. "There's a kitchen emergency. You're needed."

"Good evening to you, too." Gran wandered over, drying her hands on a towel.

He flicked a gaze her way. "Good evening. Well, Holly. Let's get a move on."

"What's the emergency?" I was already reaching for my jacket.

"Not so fast, young man." Gran stood with her hands on her hips, while Saffron growled at Chef Heston. "My granddaughter has been working hard for you all day. What gives you the right to turn up unannounced and demand she does overtime?"

"Um, well, he is my boss," I said, not keen on making Chef Heston angry. It never ended well for me.

"He could be Tutankhamen. Manners cost nothing," Gran said. "Not so much as a please or thank you, just barking orders. No wonder he's not married."

"Gran!"

She nodded. "No woman would put up with that bad behavior for long."

He grumbled under his breath. "You can have tomorrow morning off if you must. But I expect you to be back in the afternoon."

"Really?" It was rare to get an offer like that. The hours in the kitchen at Audley Castle were long and people were expected to be flexible.

"Only if you come right away," he said.

"What do you need her for?" Gran stood her ground.

"There's been a … mix up with an order for the party at Marchwood Manor. I just had word that they're short on the desserts."

"We've got plenty of options in the chiller cabinets. I can zoom some over in the van," I said.

"If it were that easy, I'd have done it myself," Chef Heston said. "Sir Richard Marchwood insisted on your special chocolate mocha cream cake. He said he'd been dreaming about it for days and was so disappointed when it didn't show up in the order."

"He should have thought about that when he put in the order," Gran said.

"He did," I said. "I remember seeing the order. He wanted thirty mini chocolate mocha cream cakes. I even wrote it on the task order for the day. Oh! Then … someone rubbed it all out."

"Really! Who would that someone be?" Gran glared at Chef Heston.

He shuffled his feet. "It's not important. We can't let our customers down."

"I think it's crucially important. Was it you by any chance, Chef Heston?" Gran said.

He grumbled several times but confessed to nothing.

I glanced at him and bit my lip. I didn't have the neatest handwriting, and Chef Heston was a stickler for everything being in order. I'd been in a hurry when I'd dashed down the tasks for the day on the board we used to check our work duties. I remembered writing down the chocolate mocha cream cake order. It was one of my favorites, and I'd planned to make an extra batch to share with Princess Alice.

Chef Heston cleared his throat. "Perhaps I did miss it off the list when I wrote out the baking tasks for the day. But Holly should have remembered."

I opened my mouth to protest, but Gran got there first. "That's not her job. You're in charge of the kitchen, and you wrote out the information incorrectly. You should make the cakes since it was your error."

"I would, but Sir Richard insists Holly does it. She's got herself something of a reputation when it comes to desserts around Audley St. Mary." Chef Heston sounded both annoyed and proud.

He should be proud. My hard work and amazing cakes reflected well on him and the castle. Not that he'd ever admit to it.

Gran smiled and threw an arm around my shoulders. "She has a magic touch when it comes to desserts. I taught her everything."

"Gran! I went to catering college."

"Well, I taught you the basics. I got you on the right track. And here you are, the queen of chocolate mocha cake in this beautiful place. You even have posh lords and ladies insisting you bake for them. They'll have you over at Buckingham Palace next, providing the desserts for the Queen."

"I'd love that. I wonder if she likes chocolate mocha cream cake," I said.

"I read somewhere she's partial to a chocolate biscuit cake," Gran said.

"I'll have to look up the recipe, just in case."

Chef Heston sighed.

I grinned. We'd let him squirm enough.

"I don't mind making the cakes," I said. "I didn't have anything planned for this evening, and we've just finished dinner."

"I suppose I can allow you to go," Gran said.

I chuckled and shook my head. "You're going on a date with Ray in half an hour. My only plans were the couch and a cuddle with Meatball. As much fun as that can be, I love any excuse to bake."

"You really need to be baking now," Chef Heston said. "The party has already started."

"The cakes won't take long to make. They'll bake quickly. I can have them over there by the time the party gets in full swing. None of the guests will miss them."

"Sir Richard missed them." Chef Heston gestured out the door.

"Because of your mistake," Gran said.

"Fine. It was my mistake. Holly, I need your chocolate mocha cream cake now."

"I'm on it." And I was always happy to help Sir Richard Marchwood. He was a kind man with a twinkle in his eye, and always generous when it came to tips. "You behave yourself on your date with Ray." I kissed Gran's cheek.

"He's always the perfect gent, no matter how much I try to convince him otherwise."

I arched an eyebrow at her. "I'm glad to hear it. He sounds like the perfect guy for you, making sure you stay on the straight and narrow."

Chef Heston tapped his foot and spent several seconds looking at his watch.

"You've made your point. Holly's coming with you," Gran said. "You can give her a minute to sort herself out."

"I'll wait outside." He slunk into the gloom.

I shrugged on my jacket, pulled on my boots, and grabbed my purse. "Meatball, do you want to stay here or come with me to your kennel?"

He was instantly up, wagging his tail. Any excuse to get outside.

"It's getting chilly out. I'll take an extra blanket so you're nice and cozy." I grabbed a few dog treats from the drawer, and an extra thick blanket that was one of his favorites, and hurried out.

Chef Heston was pacing outside, his hands twisted together. "Get a move on."

I said goodbye to Gran and then had to speed walk to catch up with him. "Do you know what the party at Marchwood Manor is for?"

"I don't question our customers why they want our desserts."

"Sir Richard is always having parties," I said. "He's really livened up the village since he bought Marchwood Manor. Didn't he move from Appledore?"

"Yes."

"That's only a few miles from here. I wonder why he moved."

"As I said, it's not my business to question customers."

"You're not the tiniest bit curious about him? His whole family seem really friendly. I don't think he's married, though."

"No, I'm not remotely curious about him. Neither should you be." Chef Heston sighed. "Not that it's your concern, but I believe it's his son having a party, not Sir Richard."

"Oh! I didn't know Jacob was home."

"You're on first name terms with Sir Richard's son?"

"Well, I don't really know him. I've met him a few times when I've made deliveries for Sir Richard. Jacob is always polite."

Chef Heston shook his head and tutted.

"What? There's nothing wrong with being nice to the customers."

"You're overly friendly. You're the same with the family."

We'd had this discussion before. Chef Heston considered me too close to the Audley family who lived in the castle. It wasn't as if I deliberately ingratiated myself with them. I'd simply clicked with Princess Alice. And as for Lord Rupert Audley, well, things were a bit more complicated there.

We walked the rest of the way in silence.

I quickly snuggled Meatball into his kennel outside the kitchen door and gave him his treats. "You be good. No barking. I won't be long, then we can go for a fun ride over to the big manor house." I dashed into the kitchen, washed up, and put on my apron.

"The oven's already heated. The ingredients are out. You just need to work your magic," Chef Heston said.

"You could help by mixing the cream." I was already measuring out flour and sugar into a large mixing bowl. I'd made my chocolate mocha cream cake so many times I could do it with my eyes closed.

Chef Heston snorted. "I'm not your commis chef. I've got work to do."

I lifted a hand. "It was just a suggestion. It could speed things up."

"I'll be in the office, sorting out the work schedule." He turned and stomped away.

Chef Heston hated being told he'd made a mistake. And he especially hated making a mistake with customers' orders. Audley Castle had an amazing reputation for creating fantastic food, and he was determined it would stay that way.

The ingredients were soon combined, and I placed the rich chocolatey mix into mini muffin tins and placed them in the oven.

I whipped the cream, cocoa powder, fresh shavings of dark chocolate, and a dash of vanilla to make the filling, then placed the bowls and mixing equipment in the industrial sized dishwasher.

The oven timer pinged. The cakes were ready. To speed things up, I left them on the side for five minutes before placing them in a chiller cabinet. If I put the cream in the cakes when they were warm, it would run right through and sit at the bottom in a sludgy lump.

While the cakes were cooling, I made thirty cream-colored miniature flowers for the decoration, and was wondering about a late night cup of tea, when Chef Heston strode back in.

"Everything ready to go?"

"Almost. I just need to put the finishing touches on the top of the cakes." I slid them into the presentation boxes and added more chocolate shavings and the tiny iced flowers.

Chef Heston peered over my shoulder. "They'll do. I've got the van out. You can drive over to the manor house."

"Are you sure? You usually make me take the bike when it's not a big order."

"We're short on time." He handed me the keys.

I was tempted to use Gran's argument and say he should make the delivery since it was his fault Sir Richard's son didn't have his cakes. But I always loved visiting Marchwood Manor. It was practically a mansion and sat on a slight hill in ten acres of pristine gardens. I also loved my job and didn't want to lose it.

"No problem. I'll zoom over there and be right back." I took off my apron and shrugged into my jacket.

"I, um, I appreciate your hard work, Holly." Chef Heston nodded at me before leaving the kitchen.

It was as close to a thank you as I was going to get, and I was happy to take it. Chef Heston had taught me a lot since I joined the kitchen at Audley Castle. Sure, he could be gruff, sometimes downright rude, and was prone to being a bit shouty, but he was a decent boss.

I opened the van, placed the cakes inside, and made sure they were secure. I whistled. "Come on, Meatball. We have a delivery to make."

He raced out of his kennel and hopped into the passenger seat of the van, while I climbed in the other side.

We were soon on our way, driving along the winding private road that led away from the castle and onto the small lanes of Audley St. Mary.

It was almost eight-thirty by the time I arrived at the manor house. It was lit up with beautiful twinkling lights around the driveway. More lights blazed from the downstairs rooms.

I parked the van close to the main door and was pulling out the boxes of cake when the door opened.

"Is that you, Holly?" Sir Richard Marchwood strolled out, wearing what must have been a custom made navy blue suit with a white shirt underneath.

"Good evening, Sir Richard. I'm here on a cake run. I heard you were missing some items from your order."

"I'm so glad you could bring them." He looked down at the glass of champagne in his hand and placed it on the window ledge. He hurried over to take the boxes.

"It's fine. I've got them."

"No, I insist. I won't stand by and see a lady fetching and carrying. Besides, I have the muscles for the job." He winked at me. "I also get a chance to nab a few cakes before my son and his greedy friends get hold of them."

I chuckled. "I don't mind doing it. It is sort of my job."

"Even so, we have to do the right thing." He took the boxes. "Sadly, I can't lay claim to all of them. Jacob's got a few of his old school friends over."

"That must be nice for him."

"I thought it would be, but the party's not going so well. There's been a couple of no-shows, and when I ducked my head in the drawing room, everyone seemed very gloomy."

"Hopefully, my cakes will cheer things up."

"As delicious as I'm sure they are, it might take more than cake to fix this social faux pas. This way." He led me into the house through the main entrance. The hallway, which was bigger than my whole apartment, was tastefully decorated with antique vases and large oil paintings of the countryside on the walls.

I followed him into an impressive granite and marble kitchen and looked around. "Would you like me to plate up the cakes?"

"Absolutely. And your timing is perfect. Most of the other nibbly bits have gone." Sir Richard tapped his fingers on the counter. "Actually, if you don't have any plans this evening, you could do more than just sort out the dessert."

I carefully placed the cakes on a plate. "Of course. What do you need? I can serve them to your guests if you want me to."

"Definitely not. I'd like you to join the party. A cheerful face is what my son needs to lighten the mood."

"Oh! I'm not sure about that. I mean …" I gestured at the cakes and then my jeans.

"Oh, Holly, you look stunning, and you'd be helping me out. I asked Jacob if there was a problem, but he said nothing was wrong. He seemed cheerful enough, but the others, well, something needs to happen, or this party will be a damp squib."

"Won't it be awkward if I simply show up?"

"Not at all. You're friendly, have a charming smile, and can woo anyone with those desserts." He winked at me again. "And I have a reputation to keep when it comes to parties. If people aren't talking about it a week after it's happened, I've done something wrong."

I bit my bottom lip. "I can't gate crash your son's party."

"He'd be thrilled to have you there. I want Jacob to enjoy himself."

The kitchen door was pushed open. Lord Rupert Audley appeared.

I was so surprised to see him, I almost dropped the tray of cakes I'd just picked up. "Hello! I didn't know you were here."

"Ah, Rupert. Come over here. I'm trying to convince the lovely Holly to join the party," Sir Richard said.

Rupert strolled over, a broad smile on his handsome face and his blue eyes sparkling. "That's the perfect idea. You must come, Holly."

"I don't really know anyone there," I said.

"You know me," Rupert said. "And have you got Meatball with you?"

"Always."

"Even better. He'll add some fun to the party. No one can resist him."

Sir Richard clapped his hands together. "Yes! Bring in your dog. Everyone will have fun petting him. We've got to do something to liven things up. What do you say, Rupert?"

"I say yes. Holly must come to the party." Rupert's grin had my resolve wavering. "Jacob won't mind you joining in. I only got an invitation at the last minute because he needed to make up the numbers."

"No! It's not just because of that. We hold your family in the highest regard," Sir Richard said. "Although the extra body definitely doesn't do any harm. I'm glad you could come."

"So am I. And the food is excellent." Rupert gestured at the tray. "Are those your chocolate mocha cream cakes I see?"

"They are," I said.

"Holly makes such incredible cakes," Rupert said.

"I know. I'm always sneaking in orders at the castle kitchen," Sir Richard said. "Holly, I insist you stay for a glass of champagne and one of your cakes. I won't hear otherwise."

Rupert caught hold of my arm and gave it a gentle squeeze. "Please stay. It would mean the world to me."

When he put it like that, I could hardly refuse. "Okay, I'll stay."

Mocha Cream and Murder is available in paperback and e-book format.

ISBN: 978-1-9163573-5-8

Here's one more treat. Enjoy this yummy recipe for beautiful blueberry muffins. Meatball and Campbell approved!

Recipe - Beautiful Blueberry Muffins

Prep time: 15 minutes **Cook time:** 25 minutes

A perfect flavorful, tender, and moist muffin to enjoy.

Store muffins in an airtight container for 3 days. Freeze for up to 2 months.

Recipe can be made dairy and egg-free. Substitute milk and yogurt for a plant/nut alternative, use dairy-free spread, and mix 3 tbsp flaxseed with 1 tbsp water to create one flax 'egg' as a binding agent (this recipe requires 6 tbsp flaxseed to substitute the 2 eggs.)

INGREDIENTS
½ cup (100g) unsalted butter, melted
2 cups (300g) plain all-purpose flour
¾ cup (150g) white granulated sugar
3 ½ tsp (18g) baking powder
2 large eggs
½ cup (130g) plain Greek yogurt
⅓ cup + 1 tablespoon (100ml) milk

1 tsp vanilla extract

2 cups fresh or frozen blueberries, if using frozen, do not thaw before adding

INSTRUCTIONS

1. Preheat oven to 425F (220C). Line a regular size 12-hole muffin pan with cases or use non-stick silicone.

2. Melt butter in the microwave for 30 seconds.

3. In a mixing bowl, add flour, sugar, and baking powder. Whisk until combined.

4. Add eggs and mix.

5. Pour in yoghurt, milk, butter, and vanilla. Fold until combined. Go gently.

6. Add blueberries and fold into mixture. Don't over mix.

7. Fill muffin cups 3/4 of the way

8. Bake for 20-25 minutes or until a toothpick inserted comes out clean.

9. Allow muffins to cool in pan for 10 minutes.

10. Transfer to a wire rack to cool (or start eating these delicious treats immediately!)

Printed in Great Britain
by Amazon